—•••—

IDENTITY THEFT

Terrorists on the Prowl

—•••—

MARY JANE FORBES

Todd Book Publications

Identity Theft

Terrorists on the Prowl

ISBN: *978-0615955339* (sc)

Printed in the United States of America
Todd Book Publications
4th Edition: 10/2017
Port Orange Florida

Website: www.MaryJaneForbes.com
Author photo: Ami Ringeisen

Cover painting: Chandler Murray, www.chandlermurray.com

Foreword

The RFID (Radio Frequency Identification) chip is used in a wide variety of ways today. Some everyday household items are embedded with chips, which can be very helpful for the manufacturer. This technology can save time during inventory, shipping, receiving, and quality control. The use of chips can help reduce the manufacturer's overall cost of goods to the consumer.

RFID chips are also being embedded into credit cards, passports, drivers' licenses, and other ID cards. This may help someone save some time by allowing them to wave these items in front of a reader instead of physically sliding the magnetic stripe through. However, the potential hazards of RFID chips being embedded into personal documentation pose risks that the general public needs to be educated about.

Identity theft as well as payment fraud is on the rise and this technology's enormous potential for abuse is rising also. If you are carrying unprotected RF data, a pickpocket no longer has to physically contact you in order to pick your pocket of information. All a thief needs in order to steal from you is a hidden reader and to get within reading range of you. Information from RFID chips can be scanned right through your wallet or purse. These readers can be freely purchased and attached to a laptop with very little technical knowledge required. Cell phones are now being created with built-in readers. How many times have you walked by someone with a cell phone or briefcase? If your personal information was stolen, how would you know where to begin your search for the culprit?

As of 2009 about 100 million credit cards now have RFID technology embedded into them. However, by the end of 2012, it is expected that credit card issuers will replace every single magnetic stripe credit and debit card with a new contactless smartcard. The RFID chip in a credit card emits the account number, expiration data and other information.

All US passports issued since October 2006 also have RFID chips in them. The chip contains all the data that is on the first page including your photo. It has been shown in various white papers that hackers can determine what country a passport has been issued from without even reading all the data on it, simply by recognizing the way the chip responds to certain scans.

While Mary Jane's book is fiction, the chance that your identity will be stolen is real. There is a simple but effective way people can protect themselves from this type of identity theft.

Some credit cards and other articles come with a layer of protection called encryption, but these layers can be broken without your knowledge. The simplest and most effective way to stop your personal information from being broadcast on the airwaves is to block the radio frequency. By placing your credit card, passport, or other ID card in a specially shielded holder, such as the Secure Sleeve®, Secure Badgeholder®, or Secure Wallet™ by Identity Stronghold, you are adding a layer of protection that you can physically see and touch.

You can take comfort that as long as your documents are inside the RFID shielded holder, an RFID reader will not be able to read the information contained on your chips. In this way, you are in control of when your personal information is read and by whom.

Walt Augustinowicz
Identity Stronghold
www.idstronghold.com

—•••—

To family and friends who encouraged
and supported me throughout the writing
of the House of Beads Mystery Series...

...this book is for you!

—•••—

Books by Mary Jane Forbes

FICTION

Bradley Farm Series
Bradley Farm, Sadie, Finn
Jeli, Marshall, Georgie

Twists of Fate Series
The Fisherman, a love story
The Witness, living a lie
Twists of Fate, daring to dream

Murder by Design, Series:
Murder by Design
Labeled in Seattle
Choices, And the Courage to Risk

Elizabeth Stitchway, PI, Series
The Mailbox, Black Magic,
The Painter, Twister

House of Beads Mystery Series
Murder in the House of Beads
Intercept, Checkmate
Identity Theft

Novels
The Baby Quilt ... a mystery!
The Message...Call Me!

Short Stories
Once Upon a Christmas Eve, a Romantic Fairy Tale
The Christmas Angel and the Magic Holiday Tree

Visit: www.MaryJaneForbes.com

Acknowledgements

The IDENTITY THEFT cover displays an original painting by Chandler Murray. Chandler is a self-taught, left-handed, youth abstract artist reminiscent of Picasso and other masters of the style. He started drawing and painting around two years old.

Highly sought after by residence and visitors to Amelia Island, Florida, his original work is featured in galleries, gift shops, TV, and newspapers in the Jacksonville and Fernandina Beach areas. The owner of Waterwheel Art Gallery on Amelia Island, Florida, says: "Chandler's art has an amazing maturity for his age and freedom of expression that ranges from the very abstract to caricatures of animals. His use of space and proportion seem natural and uninhibited."

Chandler periodically contributes his artwork to fundraising events that benefit charities, including the American Cancer Society, Habitat for Humanity, and animal rescue centers.

Chandler in his own words: "I believe art can be a very powerful form of self-expression. Art provides me opportunities for creativity; the boundaries are endless. Later in life I can see myself in graphic arts or creating animation for Pixar. In my paintings are energy, feelings, and rhythm. My favorite subject is natural science, like the world around me, animals, fossils etc. I like to paint curves and swirls. The ideas come out of my head, sometimes right before I go to sleep and then I sketch it out in my notebook and finish it the next day." Please visit Chandler's website: www.chandlermurray.com.

—•••—

Thanks to Walt and Sue Augustinowitz for providing the Foreword to this book. Identity theft is a serious issue which they delineated well. Please visit their website for more information and products to help thwart this threat: www.StrongholdID.com

Thanks to the NSERB (North Side Editorial Review Board)—Vera, Lorna, Jean, and Adele—as well as Roger and Pat Grady for struggling through the initial draft.

The bead shop, Imagine That!®, where the House of Beads Mystery Series began. Carolyn and Scott—thank you for your continued support.

—•••—

IDENTITY THEFT is the fourth and final book in the House of Beads Mystery Series.

Copper Dream Necklace

Sandra Burke, Designer

This flattering piece incorporates solid-copper findings, Crystallized Swarovksi Elements, glass beads, and crystal pears.

Materials

- 18" solid copper chain
- 5 large Vintage copper squares, drilled diagonally
- 4 10mm crystal rounds, crystal copper color
- 6 8mm crystal bicones
- 4 rectangular glass beads
- 8 6-7mm solid copper beads
- 8 10mm crystal cream pearls
- Copper head pins
- Copper clasp

Courtesy of Imagine That!®

Necklace Catherine wore to Orlando Airport on her way to Brazil.

Necklace Directions

- Determine the center of your piece of chain.

- Space out the five large copper squares around the center, determining how many links of chain you want to leave between each bead. We left three links between each bead.

- Use head pin to connect copper squares to chain— use a wire-wrap loop or a simple loop.

- Beginning with the pearls and the larger glass beads, begin to attach beads with head pin to the links between the large copper squares. Have fun with the spacing and the combinations. You can make some dangles hang lower by putting two or three beads on the head pin. Let your eye guide you!

- Finally, attach your clasp using jump rings or split rings.

—•••—

Identity Theft

Terrorists on the Prowl

—•••—

Prologue

— • • • —

HUTCH DIDN'T HEAR the siren's blare. He didn't feel the speed of the van. He didn't see the brilliance of the OR. Days later he opened his eyes. It was then he realized he had no sensation from the neck down. It was then he wished he was dead.

Six Months Later
New York City Rehabilitation Center

Hutch lifted a barbell laden with one-hundred-pound weights. Lifting the bar over his head, he performed several reps, then cursed at JJ for returning the bar to the uprights, thwarting his desire to do another set. A January snowstorm swirled outside, but Hutch's body heat was high following his workout. JJ threw him a towel to wipe the sweat from his face and neck.

Swinging from the handles of the weight-lifting machine, he settled into his wheelchair. JJ guided the chair down the hall, stepping around wet patches left along the edges of the scrubbed floor. The odor of a strong cleaner lingered in the air. Entering Hutch's private room, JJ positioned the wheelchair close to the bed, drew down the pulleys to Hutch's outstretched hands so he could hoist himself up on the bed.

Hutch still could not move his legs. He'd gained substantial improvement in his upper torso, enough so that the rehab center prescribed a rigorous workout regimen—a regimen that would return his body to its former muscular frame. The doctors felt, with any luck, he would regain at least partial use of his legs, if not all. While Hutch threw himself into rehabilitating his body, his mind remained tortured.

Three things he knew for sure. One—Catherine thought he was dead, and he was going to keep it that way. Because of him, she was almost killed during the same mission when bullets entered his body. That would not happen again. Given the nature of his profession, an undercover agent for Homeland Security, she did not need to know he survived an attack only to learn that he was shot dead the next time. He desperately wanted to learn how she was faring but never wanted to hear her name again.

Two—he was driven to regain his physical structure and mind to their original condition—critical to his uncompromising determination to expose terrorist cells in the States.

And last—never to let a woman into his heart again.

Only three people were aware he had survived his wounds suffered at the hands of terrorists bent on triggering a dirty bomb over the Belmont race track during a run for the Triple Crown—his doctor, who tried one last time to bring him back from death and succeeded; his friend JJ, who had been with him on several dangerous missions and who accompanied him to the hospital when he lay dying; and the Director of Homeland Security.

—•••—

JJ kept the director apprised of Hutch's progress. It was now time to update him. Hutch needed more than physical help—he now required mental stimulation. The kind his job as an agent provided day in and day out—the mental alertness and cunning that dangerous situations demanded.

When the director heard Hutch's body was beginning to heal, he paid him a visit. Standing outside the wall of windows of the workout room, the director watched as Hutch labored lifting the free weights. Witnessing the progress of his agent, the director knew JJ was right—it was time to talk to him about coming back to work.

After Hutch returned to his room, JJ poured him a glass of ice water. Both of them turned to see the visitor who sauntered in, pulling up a chair beside the bed.

The director, always a military man, sat ramrod straight in the chair, displaying his fit body. His demeanor and professional dress indicated a demanding management style. He raked his fingers over his shaved head—showing no hint of silver hair at the age of sixty.

"Hello, Hutchinson. That was quite a workout," the director said, leaning back in his chair. He observed the man in the bed through squinting eyes. He compartmentalized his feelings for his agents, never letting them see how much he cared about their welfare.

"Fancy seeing you here," Hutch responded glowering over at JJ. "I felt your eyes on me, but decided to ignore them. I had more important things to do, like pumping another set."

"I came to see how you were coming along. Naturally, JJ has kept me up to speed on your progress, but I wanted to witness it for myself."

"And how did you like the show?"

"Admirable. Admirable. I think it's time you come back to work."

"Can't. Pat and Mike here," he said, slapping his left, then his right thigh, "haven't paid me a visit yet."

"Your doctor believes it's only a matter of time. Have you wiggled your toes yet?"

"Nope," he answered taking a swallow of his ice water. "Actually, my big toe did salute me yesterday."

The director shrugged. "You know, Hutchinson, you've become much more important to the department since you died. Once the bad guys learned you were killed, I'm sure they crossed you off their lists as a threat. You can still work with JJ, but covertly."

"Well, that's real kind of you, but you're getting a little ahead of yourself aren't you? My legs haven't received the message that they're supposed to be moving."

"Yes, yes, perhaps. But I doubt it will be long. I've seen your determination, your spirit, more than once you know. In the meantime, you will acquire a new identity. With your permission, I'll have you transferred to a rehab center in Texas. Your assignment will be to go deep undercover. You'll join a terrorist cell we've identified that provides papers to their recruits. They enter the States through our southern and northern borders, as well as our ports. They immediately become U.S. citizens with all the credentials required to live happily ever after in the land of the free and the brave."

Hutch, sitting as upright as he could while leaning back on both elbows, looked into the director's eyes with a steely stare. "Sounds intriguing. Tell me more. Right now I'd do almost anything for a change of scene. When do you envision this little mission of yours taking place?"

"This evening...after dinner."

"Shit. The department must really be hard up for warm bodies, if you're thinking of sending a half-paralyzed man into the fray."

Ignoring Hutch's sarcasm, the director continued. "JJ will pick you up in a medical van equipped to transport you on a hospital bed. Once you're out of this facility, you'll become a German. Augustoff Weiss. Grow a mustache and a beard. JJ will accompany you to El Paso. During the flight he'll give you your new background. When you land, he'll be the male nurse who hands you off to the medics meeting the plane. JJ will leave you then, ostensibly, and you will be on your own."

"What if I have to make a run for it?" Hutch asked looking squarely into his boss's eyes at the same time patting one of his limp legs.

Again the director ignored Hutch's what-if scenario. "The facility where you'll be taken is not known as, shall we say, one of the top-rated rehab centers in the country. In fact, it's known to illegals as a place where they can take their comrades who are hurt in the border crossing with real or imaginary injuries—an underground word-of-mouth conduit so to speak. We have been led to believe, but cannot prove it, that John Doe goes in the emergency entrance of the center, and leaves by the front door as a U.S. citizen, who just happened to visit a patient there. Your mission will be to become a part of that network."

"I'll do it on one condition."

"And what is that?"

"No one, let me repeat, no one except you and JJ are to know that I survived the dirty-bomb mission. Not my mother and definitely not Catherine."

"There's something I haven't shared with you, Hutch," JJ said. "Just before Christmas, a couple of months ago, I stopped in Daytona Beach on my way back to you here in New York. By sheer coincidence, I was having dinner at a restaurant on the beach, when who should walk in but Catherine and a man. I'd never met her, but from the picture you showed me during our last mission, there is no doubt in my mind it was her."

The director caught Hutch searching JJ's face. He seemed to stop breathing. His facial muscles tightened.

"She was very pregnant," JJ said.

"Describe her dinner companion. Did he have a mustache? Was he packing a weapon?"

"I don't know about the gun, but, yes, he had a mustache, tall, about our age."

"It must have been Manny—Captain Manny Salinas, Daytona Beach PD. They knew each other in high school, and he made no pretense to hide the fact he cared deeply for her. She certainly didn't waste any tears crying over my death, now did she? So, boss," Hutch said, turning to the director, "I'm in, but in any case, Catherine is not to be told that I'm alive. Once the mission is over I'll take a long vacation and visit my mother. Try to explain why I didn't tell her before that I was alive."

"I will honor your request," the director said. He stared at the man for a few seconds. Hutch was one of his most valuable agents, and, though he would never admit it, a man he was most fond of. He wondered to himself if he was asking too much of him. But he had no choice.

Hutchinson had the perfect background to infiltrate the terrorist cell. He was multi-lingual, an expert on the computer, and had the knack of gaining the trust of those around him. The director always counted on that knack and often wondered what it was about Hutch that caused people to instantly trust him. Was it his stature—six-foot-six? Maybe. But he suspected it was his mop of dark brown hair, which always gave the appearance that he had just stumbled out of bed. Then there were his eyes—light blue and welcoming. But those eyes turned cold when assessing his opponent—human or threatening situation, or both. Yes, it was all of these, plus one more ingredient all agents must possess. He was fearless. He played the odds, in his favor or not, he didn't hesitate to go in for the kill.

"You will commit to memory my private cell number should you need it. I carry this cell with me at all times, but only a handful of operatives know of its existence. You and JJ will work out your private communication issues. However, you both must keep me updated on your progress. JJ, I want to know how to reach you at all times. Is that understood?"

"Yes, sir," JJ replied.

"Oh, there is one more thing," Hutch said. "If Pat and Mike decide not to cooperate, you and JJ will get me out of that hell hole you're dropping me into, right?"

"Agreed." The director stood, replaced the chair to its original corner, and turned to face Hutch. "Your doctor thinks you could be up and around in another three or so months and regain your muscle strength soon after, with diligent workouts, of course. During that time you'll be able to see what's going on at this so-called rehab facility, to ingratiate yourself with the staff, to see who is in on the scheme and who is not, and to plan your move to join their little charade. I'll leave you now. May you have a pleasant journey, and God bless you both."

Chapter 1

—●●●—

Nine Months Later

TRAVELERS CLOGGED the El Paso airport queuing up to check luggage, receiving boarding passes, jostling to find their way to the gates. Passengers clutching their driver's licenses and credit cards maneuvered through the check-in process. Two men and a woman, blending into the crowd, walked in different sections of the terminal's ticket counters. Each joined in one line after another, pressing close to the person in front of them or on either side. The three performed their line dance many times over a period of two hours. At the pre-determined time, and satisfied with the results of their efforts, they walked outside through the sliding glass doors.

The terminal's drop-off area was a cacophony of noises and smells—honking horns, grinding engines, buses and shuttle vans belching their exhaust fumes. Departing passengers struggled with their luggage. Airport security officials whistled and waved their arms commanding the cars move on.

A beat-up green Chevy station wagon slowed to a stop, one lane from the curb. One by one, the two men and the woman, approaching from different directions, opened the doors of the Chevy and climbed inside. The driver of the vehicle carefully merged into traffic departing the airport.

—●●●—

Rafi parked the Chevy under the carport. Pasha, Johnny and Layla piled out of the car and headed for the house on Rafi's heels. The tension of their job at the airport racked the strained muscles and brain cells of their bodies. The sharp ring of the telephone hit their raw nerves as they entered the kitchen. Rafi grabbed the phone off the wall and started pacing as he listened to the one-way conversation, only once interjecting that he was sorry he had turned off his cell and it wouldn't happen again.

Layla prepared the coffee pot and hit the on button. Pasha sat down, tilted his head back and closed his eyes blocking out the dirty yellow walls and the chipped gray-tile floor. Johnny retrieved four cups from the dish drainer, placed them on the table, and sat down next to Pasha but all the time watching Rafi.

Rafi hung up the phone, turned to look at his sister, Layla, and the two men sitting at the kitchen table. "Sayid is very unhappy with us. He says the documents we produce are poor, no better than what a child might create. If we don't improve, the test of preparing perfect identification documents will fail."

"Rafi, I told you we need help," Layla said. "I told you I know someone who can do this."

"Layla, why are you so sure?" Johnny asked. "What makes you think we can trust this person?"

"Because I know. I have tended to him for many months. He talks about his father and the family print shop in Germany. He learned the business at the knee of his father, whom he describes as a master printer."

"Ya? Well, what makes you think he'll believe in our cause?" Pasha said, grinding his cigarette butt into the ashtray.

"Stop it," Rafi yelled. "Enough. Layla, tomorrow morning, I will go with you to meet this printer. We have to do something fast or Sayid says we'll be replaced."

At ten o'clock the next morning Rafi accompanied Layla, a rehab technician, to her shift at the rehabilitation center. She took him to the workout room, which smelled of sweaty bodies trying to pump free weights, and pedaling worn looking bicycles. A man on one of the treadmills flashed her a smile, switched off the machine and carefully stepped down. Layla introduced Rafi to

Augie Weiss and suggested they talk outside. She left them to tend to others on her schedule.

In the backyard of the building, the two men found a table and a couple of weather-beaten chairs that were shielded from the warm, late morning, Texas sun.

"Layla says you know the printing business," Rafi said, lighting up a cigarette.

"I have more than a little knowledge," the man said. "As a boy in Germany, I learned from a master. His patrons required the best and trusted only him with their documents. Computers then came into the picture. My father wasn't able to make the adjustment and that's when I really began to learn the trade. Layla said you and she are in the printing business."

"Yes. My sister and I are looking for someone who knows the new printer technology. What we are producing is not good enough. It must be the best, but there are special circumstances."

"Hell. That's all I've heard for the past year—special circumstances. 'You have to leave this New York hospital. We've done all we can and now it's up to you. We have to have the bed for more critically wounded military personnel.' They gave me a list of three rehab centers. I chose the one farthest away from New York."

"What did they mean by military personnel?"

"I was wounded on an assignment as a freelance photographer for Der Spiegel. You know, the news outfit. Being a German American, the military sent me to the States to tend to my wounds. Now this rat hole tells me I'll be discharged in a week. A week! I have no money, no job, and no place to stay. You know what I think? I think for all their high-minded talk, the staff hates German Americans. Well, I don't like them either."

"What about returning to Germany?" Rafi asked.

"Germany? I will never return to Germany. My parents hated it. Why else would they leave? But then they hated America, too— horrible, uncaring people. My parents made sure I became a citizen and then left me to struggle through college. They returned to Germany—better than the U.S. they now thought."

"Maybe we can help each other, that is if you're as good as you say. If not, we go our separate ways."

"Shit, I don't have anything to lose. I need money, a job. No harm in giving it a try, I guess."

"Why don't you come for supper tonight? I'll show you a sample of what we do for the government."

"Government?"

"Yes, we do special work for new Americans."

Chapter 2

— • • • —

"GODDAMN IT, leave me alone. I'm working as fast as I can. You can't rush these documents or they won't look authentic," Augie yelled. "Now get out of here."

The door slammed shut behind the intruder leaving a whoosh of air behind. Irritated at the intrusion, Augie returned his attention to the computer monitor sitting on a makeshift desk consisting of a scarred wooden door supported on each end by dented, two-drawer, gray-metal file cabinets. The one window filtered the sunlight through streaks of dirt, but it didn't matter because the overhead fluorescents lit up the small space jammed with computer equipment, printers, and supplies, like an operating room.

Augie downloaded the latest RFID scans the group had harvested at the airport earlier in the day—more than they had anticipated for the second week in January. They called themselves farmers. All they needed to pick up information transmitted from documents embedded with radio frequency identification chips was a special antenna and a scanner. With this equipment they went to the airport, sometimes a train or bus station, strolled around the area scanning for the information transmitted by the chips. They then returned to the farmhouse with their harvest. With the scanned files, Augie was charged with the additional responsibility to find all the personal information he could about the individuals from their passports, driver's licenses, and credit cards—intelligence captured if their documents contained the RFID chips.

Some people were easy targets. They foolishly revealed confidential material on social websites like Twitter and Facebook, which then lead to other sites, sometimes where resumes were posted. Others took time to gain their full names, addresses, and social security numbers. The credit cards easily displayed all the information needed to complete a transaction. If Augie was really lucky and found extensive personal information by searching the internet, he could produce a complete background for an illegal pretending to be someone else. Of course, that was just the beginning. He then set to work with his sophisticated software to precisely reproduce the new identity documents—a new social security card and driver's license with picture were mandatory.

After several hours bent over his desk in sustained concentration, Augie stood, stretched, performed a couple of knee bends—well over a year-and-a-half since he was shot, he still suffered aches in his legs if he remained in one position for any length of time. Working with the scanned files Rafi had given him, he was still amazed at the information the scanner picked up from the so-called contactless smart cards—no hit on the head to rob someone. Hell, stealing someone's identity was as easy as a stroll in the park. The radio waves transmitted by the embedded RFID chips could be picked up by a thief drinking a latte next to you or, in some cases, fifty feet away. Feeling the pressure to finish the batch of documents, Augie returned to his computer.

A soft knock on the door preceded the entrance of a woman. Augie caught the scent of her perfume but did not look away from his computer.

"Augie, you work so hard," Layla said. "Come, take a break." She encircled his shoulders with her arms. Laying her cheek on his thick brown hair, she moved to kiss him tenderly on the tip of his ear.

"Layla, not now," Augie said, gently pushing her hand away from his neck. "I have to make at least three sets of documents. Rafi is expecting a visitor tomorrow morning. He told the man the papers would be ready in time for his return flight to Detroit."

"Well, I want to share some news with you," she said, rubbing his temples, "but if you are too busy—"

"What news?" He turned in his chair putting his arms around her thin waist.

"Well," she said, pausing to give him a soft kiss on his lips, "Johnny has left the farm."

"What do you mean he's left the farm? He's going to join another group?" Augie asked.

"No, I don't think that's what Rafi meant. He said Johnny screwed up. He broke one of the rules. Rafi said he's gone for good." Layla leaned in to give Augie a more passionate embrace. Lifting her head she continued, "And, Rafi said we are going to move our operation to the east coast."

"Where on the east coast? Not back to New York!" Augie stood, carefully untangling himself from the woman, taking hold of her arms, moving her away, and holding her there.

"Augie, don't push me away. I promise not to disturb what you're doing." She again moved closer to him, playing with a lock of hair on his forehead. "I just wanted to let you know we're going to a very beautiful place, Amelia Island. Rafi says it's just south of the Georgia border."

"You mean Florida?"

"Yes," she said, kissing his forehead lightly.

"When are we supposed to make this move?"

"Rafi said soon. Maybe you and I will have more time together. I would like that." Layla leaned into him, her dark eyes burning into his, begging him to kiss her.

"That is interesting news. Now I have to get back to my work," he said, giving her a peck on the cheek, a pat on her bottom, and stepping back to his computer with barely a limp. *That's just great,* he thought. *Exactly what I don't want. I'll be within spitting distance of Catherine and her new husband.*

Chapter 3

—••••—

CATHERINE, A FEW months from turning thirty-eight, rounded her assistant's desk and headed for a small conference room. She was chic as ever in a light gray suit, punctuated by a white silk blouse with a deep V neckline. Ever mindful of the vagaries of the Florida humidity even in January, she wore her hair in a tight twist anchored by three pearl hairpins. Her signature necklace, a gold St. Christopher medal, lay softly on her tan skin, the medal that her lover had given her four days before he was killed.

Catherine paused to look over her office complex from the fourth floor balcony. Her firm, of which she was now president, continued to prosper but remained an international architectural and design firm at its core. But because of the growing profits the company was generating, she was now able to fund two spinoff businesses. These two startups were the subject of the meeting she was about to chair.

"Hello, everyone. Hearing your chatter, it sounds as if you're all in good spirits this morning," Catherine said, helping herself to coffee and adding a thimble of cream.

"I was just reminding my dear friend, Fred here, that the Jaguars have the best quarterback in the league," Pete said.

"And, knowing Pete's love of a wager, I bet that the Jags would win this Sunday but only by three points. If they win by more than three, I'll treat him and Tillie with tickets to their next home game, plus ten bucks on the side." Fred pushed a ten dollar bill into the center of the table.

"Brenda, have you settled on a Florida team yet?" Catherine asked, enjoying the byplay of her most trusted friends, and heads of her two new divisions in the company.

"It's hard. One week it's the Dolphins, but then I, along with Pete, really like the Jags."

"Just be glad, Brenda, as Vice President of Operations, you don't have to manage a football team. Not yet anyway." Catherine's eyes sparkled at the shocked look on their faces. They never knew what she was going to get them into next.

She was thankful that Pete and Tillie, co-heads of the Bead & Cyber Café Franchise Division, were in the country for today's meeting. Pete fell head over heels in love with Tillie the moment Catherine introduced them. And, truth be told, Tillie felt the same way. Catherine had wanted his advice, and hopefully his help, in establishing a cyber café as an extension of Tillie's bead shop. Now, less than two years later, the scheme was thriving, as well as their recent marriage. With Pete's cyberspace expertise and Tillie's artistic designs, knowledge of beads, and the growing bead jewelry business, Catherine had offered the combination as a franchise to prospective buyers. She hired the two of them to manage and grow the enterprise as a division of her firm.

"Now, let's get—"

"Now, just one minute there, madam chairwoman. How is that darling little boy of yours?" Pete asked.

"That *darling* little boy is into everything. If I thought he constantly found himself in trouble crawling, now that he's begun to walk it's amazing how quickly he disappears from one room to the next," Catherine said taking her seat at the head of the black lacquer conference table and looking up at her two friends. "Now, you two, please give us your report. How are your negotiations going in China?"

"I'll let my darlin' Tillie give you her side of the shop first," Pete said with a wink at Catherine.

"It's very exciting," Tillie said. Unable to contain her enthusiasm, she stood to address the group. A slip of a woman in her mid-forties, her vivid blue eyes were shining with excitement. "As you know, Pete and I just returned from Beijing. What a bustling city that is. We had the most wonderful interpreter, and he agreed to help us through the morass of regulations and licenses that the Chinese government requires. For a fee, of course."

"That doesn't sound very exciting," Fred chimed in. "The fee part."

"Oh, it isn't. It's positively dreadful," Tillie replied. "But the beads we found were exquisite. On the flight home, Pete and I brainstormed how we can rearrange the shop's layout to feature beads from various countries. But wait, I'm getting ahead of myself. I believe we can satisfy all the Chinese regulations in about six months."

"Catherine, you've turned my Tillie into a hard-nosed negotiator," Pete said. "She's just so adorable, that I know the Chinese agent thought he could pull the white downy feathers of the egret over her eyes. Well, he had another thing coming."

"Oh, Pete, you're just prejudice," Tillie said, retaking her seat, a slight flush creeping over her face framed by soft brown curls.

"Pete, I guess that's your cue. I see you're using your wheelchair today. Anything the matter with your legs?" Catherine asked.

"No, no. I wore my shapely titanium limbs too much in China, so the stumps are a little sore. Nothing a few days on my keister won't fix."

"That's a relief," Catherine said. She always kept a watchful eye on Pete, one of her favorite people. She felt a strong connection with him—her lover's best friend. They had served together in Iraq where Pete stepped on an IED losing both legs below the knee. Once he met Tillie, however, he abandoned his wheelchair preferring to walk as he courted her. He now wore his prosthetics most of the time and enjoyed tootling her around in his red Thunderbird.

"Where Tillie ran into one roadblock after another," Pete continued, "the agent seemed to defer to me—anxious to cut the red tape for the cyber cafes. The Chinese are enamored with computers, yet many don't have them in their homes. There are a few local cyber cafes, but none with the whole setup we'll be offering. Of course, we come as a package deal—they don't get the cafes without the beads," Pete said, patting Tillie's hand.

"So you both think it will be six months before you can start laying out the shops?" Catherine asked.

"Yes," Pete said, "but that doesn't mean we won't hit the ground running. We've already found two locations and are negotiating with both bead and computer dealers. So, all the upfront work will be done by the time we get the green light."

"Well, of course, the shop in London has turned out to be a big success," Tillie interjected. "We're looking at New Delhi, and possibly Nairobi. The women wear incredibly colorful necklaces. They really are beautiful. I think when we bring China online, and if we find we can open in Kenya without worrying about becoming entangled in any unrest, we should write an article about our beads. More than the press releases we've been sending out. Maybe pass it by Oprah's people to see if she'll run a feature story in her magazine."

"Oh, I love that idea." Catherine made a few notes on her yellow pad of paper and then turned to Fred.

"Fred, I saw your document outline, but fill me in on your ideas for a personal security business."

"Well, as you know, Brenda urged me to make a proposal to you for a new division—offering a personal and corporate security service. With the threat of terrorism a major issue in the U.S. we know such a service is going to be in demand, in fact, it already is."

"Tell me, have you said anything to your boss?" Catherine asked.

"Yes, I have. I would never do anything behind Manny's back. As Captain of the Daytona Beach Criminal Investigation Division, and as a friend, he's been very good to me. In fact, I hope he'll join us, but so far he says he likes it where he is. Doesn't cotton to the shirt and tie scene," Fred chuckled.

"I see," Catherine said looking down at the yellow tablet in front of her. "Well, maybe in time he'll change his mind. On the other hand, I know he's a dedicated officer." Tillie and Pete, and Brenda and Fred exchanged quick glances. It was known to them, as well as Catherine, that Manny had strong feelings for her. He probably felt he couldn't be so close to her every day, and yet not as close he wished to be.

"The business plan is almost complete," Fred said. "My contact, at the firm Mayor Giuliani started after 9/11, has been very helpful, as well as a couple of agents from Homeland Security Brenda knew when she handled some of the computer forensic investigations for them. I'm having some problems recruiting a team, or maybe it's just because I'm being too picky. But I don't think so. We want the very best security experts we can find, and they must be multi-lingual. I suggest we start offering the service in the States, but, once we're up and running, I want to be able to branch out into hot spots around the world. I know this is a once-in-a-lifetime business opportunity you've offered me. Given the dangerous times we live in, strategically, the timing is perfect to offer a security service to both individuals as well as corporations."

Fred was recruited to the Daytona Beach PD from New Mexico, where he worked on the border patrol. He still carried the scars from apprehending illegals crossing the border into the States. The day he joined the border patrol, he went into his bathroom and shaved the Afro-style hair off his head. He still maintains his bald head.

"I for one find your ideas very exciting," Catherine said. "Now, I have a couple pieces of news to share with you. First of all, I received an email today from Russell. He's in Brazil."

"How's he doing after handing the reins of Stone & Associates over to you?" Brenda asked.

"Quite well...I think. In the past two years, he seems to have gotten his bearings. I'm sure he still mourns the death of his wife. Such a senseless, tragic death. The murder of your wife at the hands of your arch rival is not something you come to grips with overnight. Anyway, I receive an email once in a while from various locations. This one, however, makes me think he truly is starting to become his old self. He wanted to let us know about a potential business opportunity. It seems a big development is being proposed for a beach in Rio de Janeiro. He sees it as a duplicate of the multiplex he headed up here in Daytona Beach. The project, I might add, that catapulted this architectural and building firm into prominence worldwide." Catherine paused to take a sip of her coffee. "He wants me to fly to Rio to take a look at it, but I just don't see how I can get away. We have so many irons in the fire right now. And then there's little Stephen's birthday party. Can you believe it, he'll be one next week."

Brenda leaned over, putting her hand on Catherine's. Brenda was with her at the birth of her son, a wonderful but bittersweet time. In fact, everyone in the room shared in welcoming little Stephen into the world that night.

"Hey now, you listen to me, Catherine Hainsworth," Pete said. "After little Stephen's birthday party, which by the way you'll have to build a barn to house the pony I'm giving him—"

"Pete," Catherine said, mocking him with a stern face, "you'd better be kidding."

"I didn't say how big a barn. It's a rocking horse, silly," Pete laughed. "Anyway, why don't you take the little one with you to Brazil? I'm sure his nanny would be more than happy to accompany you. I can just see Lucy with the tot. She's so devoted to him."

"Well, it's a thought. I'll mull the idea over with her. Now, the last item on the agenda is the change in the company name. Brenda, how do things stand?"

"I spoke with the lawyer yesterday, and all the paperwork is done. The fees for the changes are paid, so, as of the first of February, we will be known as the Daytona Beach Corporation. Signage on the building outside, as well as inside, website, stationery, and all the company forms will display the new name. I know you've been discussing this for a long time," Brenda said, "but now that it's official, how does Russell feel about the change?"

"He thinks it's very appropriate given the various divisions we now have under one umbrella. As he said, 'who knows what we'll come up with next?' We've come a long way together haven't we?" Catherine said, smiling at Brenda.

She and Brenda had become very close. She looked to her as a sister. They were a striking pair when they walked around the company together, or a restaurant, or around town—Catherine an attractive blonde, Brenda a beautiful black woman with creamy chocolate skin and shoulder length, silky black hair. Both women were close to the same height with Brenda just a couple of inches taller at five-foot-six. Of course, high heels were generally part of their corporate uniform. At home, bare feet or sandals prevailed. Catherine invited her to share her home when she first moved to Daytona Beach from DC. Brenda was the VP of Information Technology at the time, reporting to Russell Stone before he retired. It was at that time Russell had handed the entire operation of the company over to Catherine. Detective Fred Watson slipped a diamond on Brenda's finger about six months ago and the two had become inseparable. Brenda now spent more time at Fred's house than she did with Catherine. Catherine thought they were a perfect match and cared deeply for them both.

— ••• —

"Lucy, I'm home. I'll be right up to give Stephen his bath and tuck him in for the night." Catherine ran up the first flight of stairs to her bedroom, quickly changing into her jeans. She took the pearl hairpins from her twist, letting her blonde hair fall softly to her shoulders. Leaving her feet bare, she walked across the hall to the nursery. Stephen was standing in his crib watching for her to come through the door.

"Hello, my little man. Have you been a good boy for Lucy today?" she said smiling, lifting him out of the crib, hugging him tight.

"He's been a very good boy, Miss Catherine. We went to the park today. Tell your mama what you saw, Stephen."

Stephen looked from Lucy to his mother, and then back to Lucy.

"Did you see an elephant?" Lucy asked.

"Yeth," he replied holding his arms wide to show Catherine the elephant was very big.

"Sounds like fun. Lucy, I'll give Stephen his bath, and after tucking him in I have something I want to talk over with you."

— ••• —

Stephen always enjoyed his bath. He seemed to understand that this was a special time with his mama. Catherine usually had to change her T-shirt because, with all the splashing and laughing, she ended up soaking wet. Finishing up, she carefully lifted him from the tub, wrapping him in a towel. Carrying him to his crib, they both giggled as she tried to get his jammies on his squirming body. Finally succeeding, Stephen laid down looking over to the chest by his bed, waiting for his mother to wind the key to start the music and to give his daddy's picture a kiss.

He was never disappointed. *Lullaby and Goodnight* played softly in the dim light as Catherine picked up Hutch's picture, kissed it softly, and whispered, "Good night, my agent. I love you."

Chapter 4

—•••—

"AUGIE, WHY CAN'T I go with you?" Layla slithered onto his lap blocking the computer screen.

"I told you. I'll only be gone a little while. I have to meet with our dealer. Order the supplies to last until we leave El Paso and enough to set up after the move—you'd be bored. Now scoot, so I can get my work done."

"Okay, but be as quick as you can. You know I'll miss you."

Ignoring her last statement, Augie said, "I told Rafi where I'm going. I'll be back before dinner."

Augie left the ramshackle house they were renting, hopped on his old Harley, and headed into another rundown area of the city. He pulled into the parking lot of an abandoned building. Retrieving his cell from his khaki cargo pants, he called JJ.

"Are you close by?"

"Affirmative."

"I'll be under the oak tree in one hour. Can you make it?"

"Yes. Want a beer?"

"What's this *A beer*? Make it two, shithead."

Augie roared out of the weed-infested parking lot and headed to his dealer. After arriving at the shop, he gave the owner his order and explained that he and his friends were moving east, to Florida, on the border with Georgia. Augie asked the man if he might be able to give him a steer for a like-minded dealer where he could purchase his special supplies. Luckily the man thought he might have a contact in the Jacksonville area. "I'll let you know for sure when you come back to pick up your order."

"Thanks. I appreciate your help," Augie said as he pulled on his helmet.

"I'm just sorry to lose such a good customer," the dealer said, picking up the order slip marked with the scribbles he had added, as Augie left the shop.

Making sure the dealer had the order correct took a little longer than Augie anticipated, so he had to step on it to get to the park on time. He did his usual double-back maneuver to ensure he was not being tailed. Driving up to a set of swings, he saw a mother pushing her two little boys squealing that she push them higher. The smell of fresh mown grass filled his nostrils as he watched the children. *Such a peaceful scene,* he thought. *I wonder if I'll ever be able to take a child to the park...without looking over my shoulder.*

Other than the woman and her children, the playground area of the park was empty. He spotted a man lying on a bench. His six-foot-four body covered the full length of the boards. A newspaper shielded his face, tent style. If the bald man lifted the corner of the paper, he could see the gravel parking area where Augie parked his bike. A large oak tree stood about thirty feet away from the bench. Augie went around to the other side of the tree, the trunk so large that if anyone drove into the parking area they would not see him. Two beers were leaning against the side of the tree.

"How're you doin', partner?" JJ asked his cell shielded from sight by the back of the bench as well as the *El Paso Times*. "You look pretty darn good all things considered. It's been a year and a half since your little run in with those nasty bullets. Are your legs giving you any trouble?"

"Once in a while. Mainly just tired muscles if I stand or sit in one position too long. But it's this woman, Layla, whose giving me a real problem—a dark Pakistani woman. She keeps coming on to me. If she wasn't Rafi's sister I'd tell her to buzz off. But I can't risk it."

"Why can't I get an assignment like that? No beautiful woman for me. No. I get to watch your sorry ass," JJ countered.

"Did I say she was beautiful? Enough of this. Listen up. I have some information for you to pass on to big daddy."

"Shit and I thought you just wanted to see me, share a beer, swap horror stories."

"Ya, well I have a horror story in the making, if you'll let me get a word in edgewise. By the way, next time bring me a lime...cut up. I don't want to dirty my little pocketknife."

"Yes, sir. Now give me what you got."

"First, they seem to like my work. Their trial of harvesting the ID's at the airport has gone smoothly, and I've been able to find personal, as well as background information, on the people they've nailed. Hell, get this. Rafi ordered the antennae and the scanner from eBay for 197 bucks, everything he needed to pick up radio frequency waves from unsuspecting travelers whose documents had the RFID chip embedded."

"You're kidding me. What a deal."

"It's been so successful, and with my print production, they have decided to go into full operation. Their mission is for us to be a supplier of documents needed to turn an illegal crossing the border into Joe Citizen, and in some cases the reverse—a U.S. citizen who needs a new identity to join a terrorist cell. They are ramping up their recruiting efforts for what mischief I don't know yet. From the ID's they've harvested the terrorists cells will look like the United Nations, no profiling here. Everyone is welcome to join."

"Clever how you keep using the word harvest," JJ said.

"Oh, right. The operation is referred to as a farm. The members who go out with their eBay scanning equipment are called farmers. They are going out to harvest their crops. Sometimes they refer to males as beanstalks and brussels sprouts or parsley for women. Beanstalks are preferred."

"That would be my preference," JJ chuckled. "I've hated brussels sprouts ever since my mother made me eat one. I showed her—I threw up."

"JJ, shut up. This is serious business."

"Okay, just trying to bring a little levity into your pitiful life."

"Rafi said we're leaving El Paso in a week. I just came from negotiating the deal for our special paper we use for passports, social security IDs and the parts for driver's licenses. I had to get the order in so we have everything before we move the operation. He asked me to be ready to continue processing the documents immediately after we move. I also asked the dealer to locate someone at the other end for me. Otherwise, I'm not sure how long it will take to find another outfit with the special stuff we need."

"Where are we going, partner?"

"Amelia Island."

"Where the hell is Amelia Island?" JJ asked.

"Florida. About fifteen minutes north of Jacksonville. It's almost on Georgia's border."

"Oh, no. Anywhere but Florida. I'm sorry—you'll be so close, yet far away from her."

"Hey, what do I care? I have Layla, who wants yours truly, remember? It doesn't matter to me if I'm in Florida or not."

"Um, sure, right. You don't care."

"There's more. I'm sending you pictures from my cell phone of my four farmer friends. Check 'em out. Rafi is the clean cut guy. Pasha has the clipped black beard, and Layla is, well, Layla. The fourth man is, or was Johnny. Layla was the first to tell me, after they had returned from a harvest, that Johnny was gone. She said Rafi told her that Johnny broke one of the farm's rules. When I asked Rafi later in the day where Johnny was, he just said he left and would not be coming back...ever. He added that 'if someone is caught breaking the farm's rules, he will not see the sun again.'"

JJ scanned the pictures Augie just sent him on his cell phone to be sure he had the identities right. "Whoa, Layla is some dish, and that body doesn't stop. You'd better watch yourself, bro," JJ chided.

"Not my type. Also, they only go by their first names. I'm sure Layla gave Rafi my last name because she recruited me from the rehab center. Weiss was noted on the clipboard at the foot of my bed. Tell the director that I'm keeping a record of all the documents I produce for the department's files. I'll send the list to you after each batch is processed. One more thing, I put a bug in Rafi's briefcase, i n the lining. When we get to Amelia Island, I'll bug the whole damn house—telephone, car, kitchen, living room, and wherever they assign me to set up the printing equipment."

"Well, be careful. You're the only outsider, the new kid on the block so to speak, so they'd probably shoot you on the spot if they find the bugs. No questions asked."

Chapter 5

—•••—

RAFI TRADED IN the Chevy for a van so they could ride more comfortably on their 1700 mile trip from El Paso to Amelia Island. They were going from one warm climate to another, practically in a straight line from west to east. Traveling light, the group of four still needed a U-Haul trailer. The most important part of the items they were transporting was their sophisticated computer and printing equipment, and the load of supplies Augie had ordered. His dealer had come through with an establishment in Jacksonville where, he was told, they would be more than happy to fulfill his needs.

The weather was pleasant as Rafi navigated along Interstate 10 heading east. Augie took advantage of the relaxed camaraderie in the van to try to learn more about his companions. He had relayed Rafi and Pasha's physical description to JJ. They both had black hair and dark eyes, and were very muscular men. While Rafi was a clean-shaven Pakistani, Pasha's face was covered with a thick black beard, which he meticulously clipped short. But the two had not been forthcoming with their backgrounds.

"Rafi, how did you and Pasha meet?" Augie asked gazing out the window at the Gulf waters along the Louisiana coastline.

"A most raucous place, aye, Pasha? We literally bumped into each other in a bar on the border of Pakistan and Afghanistan. We quickly found we had a common cause—hatred of the United States and the western world in general. When Pasha and I decided to take the fight to the enemy, and travel to the States, Layla tagged along seeking adventure. She didn't care if it was in the States, somewhere in Europe, or Asia."

"Layla, have you found adventure?" Augie asked still gazing out the window.

"Oh, yes. And I hope what I dream comes true."

"How did you two men come to start the first farm?"

"One of my close contacts in Pakistan recruited me. He told me of his scheme to steal identities of U.S. citizens and give them to recruits who entered the States through various clever methods, or to disgruntled Americans joining our cause. The new members, of course, would share our ideology."

The van continued to travel east and the occupants fell into a comfortable silence, a silence filled with their own thoughts.

Augie knew from his initial conversation with Rafi that a critical member of his team had been missing—someone with the knowledge and experience that could be adapted to reproducing the documents they needed. Then Layla, employed part-time at the rehab center in El Paso, became fond of him and helped him as he worked diligently to walk again. She nursed him back to health, at least in her mind, and Augie let her think this and fed her the information about his background. He led her to discover that he had the talent the farm was looking for. Augie soon learned that Rafi, her brother, was the head of the group he was charged to find. Now as a critical member of the group, the testing of the scheme completed, they were leaving Texas to set up the operation in the southeast.

— • • • —

It was dark when the rented white van, pulling the trailer, slowed to a stop. The moon spotlighted the causeway ahead joining the mainland with Amelia Island.

"We've made excellent time," Rafi said. "By making only one stop we are ahead of schedule. I suggest we stay the night at the motel we passed about a mile back. Then we'll head into town and our rental house in the morning. The beds won't be made up anyway and we don't want to look like we're sneaking around in the middle of the night—we want to appear friendly, neighborly even."

"That sounds good, Rafi," Layla said, yawning. "I'm exhausted. I don't want to be cooped up in this van another minute."

"You know, my legs are cramping. I'd like to stretch as well," Augie said. "And Pasha's been squirming like a kid for the last two hours."

"Worry about yourself, Augie. I'm doing just fine, but I sure don't want to unload tonight," Pasha snapped.

Rafi carefully maneuvered the van around and headed back to the motel. He booked two rooms, one for the men, and one for Layla.

"Layla, be ready by 7:30," Rafi ordered. "We'll have breakfast in the little café we passed, grab some extra coffee, drive to our new house and become productive citizens of Amelia Island."

"I can't wait to see the house you rented," Layla said. "With a little shop in front, it's perfect to set up a copying and photo printing service for tourists as well as the locals. I'm excited about helping, and I know I can operate the equipment. You did say all I had to do was push some buttons, right?"

"That's right," Rafi said chuckling. "A push-button operation."

"So, I'll be able to man the shop, except when we need to do more harvesting," she giggled.

They went to their rooms, settling in for the night. Layla, wishing Augie was with her and not in the next room, was restless and stepped outside on their second-floor walkway. "Rafi, you can't sleep either?"

"Just going over my list of things to do tomorrow. What has you roaming around?"

"Augie. You know I like him, yes?"

"I'd say it's more than that."

"Rafi, he doesn't look at me, you know, like a man who wants me. I hope this new house will help him see me differently."

"Be patient. You're a very pretty woman—he'll come around. Maybe talk about a family. Once we settle down in the house, he may see you as a woman who can give him a home. A man likes that...especially when he starts thinking about making a family with a woman as beautiful as you."

"Oh, I never thought of it that way. What an insightful brother you are," she said throwing her arms around him, giving him a quick hug.

—•••—

After breakfast the next morning the group piled back into the vehicle. Rafi drove over the causeway into the historic, tree-lined center of Fernandina Beach. The quaint town looked like a storybook southern village from times past.

"Oh, look, Augie, at all the little shops. This is going to be so much fun," Layla said, leaning forward in her seat.

Rafi and his gang looked out the van's windows from side to side at arching trees lining the narrow side streets. The colorful homes restored and freshly painted in pale colors of green, blue, and pink, like the day they were built—the trim in white or a contrasting color of the house. Many of the homes had wrap-around verandas, providing a cool retreat when the days were hot.

Turning down a side street, the van pulled to a stop in front of a two-story Victorian house. The right-hand side had been converted into a shoe repair shop, which was now out of business. The proprietor of the shop had rented the house hoping to buy it when his business took hold. Unfortunately, his dream did not come true. The owner of the house was thrilled when Rafi said it would be perfect for his family and the photo supply shop he planned to open. Without asking for anything more than the first and last month's rent, he had handed the keys to Rafi. The owner was pleased to have a nice, quiet, family business take up residence in his rental property.

Chapter 6

— • • • —

A FEW DAYS LATER having settled quickly in the house, the members of the team huddled for a late breakfast in the small garden warmed by the February sun. Layla put out warm buns, soft butter, orange marmalade jam, and a few apple slices along with a fresh pot of coffee. She enjoyed going to the little bakery around the corner, walking to purchase their baked goods every chance that came her way.

"About an hour ago, I received an email from Sayid, our leader," Rafi said. "Now that our equipment is set up, he wants us to proceed—harvesting, researching, producing the documents— in other words, start full operation. By the way, Augie, he commends you on your work. He said the documents in the package you sent before we left El Paso were the best he'd ever seen."

"Good to hear," Augie replied, breaking open a bun, dipping it in the jam, and washing it down with a swallow of coffee. "When do I get to meet this guy, Sayid?"

"Perhaps in a few weeks, maybe less," Rafi said. "In fact, he may bring a couple of new recruits, new farmers for harvesting. He hoped they would be good enough to operate a farm. But so far, he's not very happy with them. He thinks they should take a lesson from you."

"Anything I can do to help the cause. Just let me know ahead of time so I can dust the office," Augie said with a chuckle.

"Come on, Rafi. Stop with the chitchat," Pasha said. "What was in those emails you received? I hope we're going to resume harvesting. I'm getting tired of this place. Too confining."

"Oh, stop your complaining, Pasha," Layla said. "This is a wonderful place. I love the shops, and the people are very friendly."

"You'll be happy to hear, Pasha, that we are to resume harvesting," Rafi said. "However, we are not to be the only farm. Sayid informed me he is in the process of setting up three more farms. He used the last of the documents you sent to him, Augie. Each farm will have three harvesters. They will be located at first in Detroit, New York, and Tucson. We are to work out of Orlando."

"Just who is going to prepare the documents for all these farmers?" Augie asked looking intently at Rafi, a scowl crossing his face.

"Funny you should ask, my friend. You are," Rafi said.

"Bullshit," Augie said slamming his empty orange juice can down on the wooden picnic table. It takes me a long time to do the research, to say nothing about finding resumes and building backgrounds." He jumped up, rubbing his brown hair which had grown almost to shoulder length. "Did Sayid give you a clue as to how I'm supposed to handle the extra load?"

"Calm down, Augie. That is one reason he's bringing the potential farm captains here. You are to show them what you do and discuss what kind of help you need. In the short term, we will handle everything from here. Depending on how things go, you will either remain here, transfer to another farm, or simply aid in duplicating our operation in other locations. In the meantime, Pasha, Layla, and I will handle the research on the internet while you pull together and print the documents."

"Oh, I like that," Layla said. "I will help you, Augie. We will work well together don't you think? Rafi, if Augie travels to another farm, I can go with him, yes?"

"Not now, Layla, and for God's sake don't mention such a thing to Sayid," Rafi said with a stern look at his sister. "You know, he's not happy you came with me. So I think it best if you keep quiet."

"Well, I'll need all three of you to help with the research, that's for sure," Augie said. "And, I'm going to have to change my morning routine. If I'm going to be hunched over my work table and printer, to say nothing of the computer, then I'm going to need to get out, get some exercise. Running has always helped me relax, get the kinks out. Now that my legs are stronger, it's about time I started. I've just been lazy since I was pushed out of the rehab center. With the beach a couple miles down the road, greeting the sunrise will help. Excuse me, I'm going to the electronics store and pick up a light-weight radio so I can block out you guys bickering over the research detail."

"When you get back, I say let's go out for a late lunch," Rafi offered. "How about the Happy Tomato? It's warm enough so we should be able to sit out in their garden."

— • • • —

Augie, still scowling, went into the house to wash up. He spent the following half hour looking over what the little store on Centre Street had to offer. He bought a two-way radio with headphones. The unit also picked up the local radio station that played music twenty-four seven. When he returned, he joined Rafi and Pasha standing in the shop waiting for Layla to turn off the copy machines. She put the closed sign in the door window as they left, and walked quickly to catch up with Augie, taking hold of his hand.

"Augie, I like the new plan. It will work. You'll see." Giving his hand a squeeze, she looked up at him with her warm dark eyes.

"We'll see," he said, removing his hand from hers to swat an imaginary bug off his shirt.

— • • • —

Oh, Augie, Layla thought. *I'm so in love with you. How am I going to make you understand how happy we will be working together...working closely together...as a couple? Rafi was right, maybe even someday with a baby...a real family.* She stole a sideline glance at him, taking his hand once more as they entered the restaurant, leaning into his body as he held the door for her.

Chapter 7

—•••—

THE HORIZON BEGAN to brighten to a hint of light gray, as the surf ushered in a rising tide. The moon was still visible. A lone man sat on the sand. Leaning forward, he tapped his knees in rhythm to the music streaming softly through his earpiece. There was a white plastic bag on the sand between his feet.

Another man approached jogging from the north. He stopped beside the man with the headphones. Holding his arm out, he appeared to be checking his watch and in the process dropped his towel. He wadded up his towel, nodded to the sitting man, and continued jogging south down the beach. Seeing a stand of bushes where the sand ended, the jogger stopped for a rest, sitting down on the cool sand. Unfolding the towel, now wrapped around a white plastic bag, he dug out the contents stuffing the items into his left- and right-leg pockets. There was a piece of paper in the bottom of the bag. "My number is taped to the bottom of your radio. It has a range of thirty-six miles. Call me. Now. Love and kisses, Augie."

—•••—

A smile crossed JJ's face as he pushed the plugs into his ears and punched in the number he was given.

"Took you long enough," Augie said. "How's the reception?"

"Like you're standing next to me. It's a great radio—small yet no static. I haven't played walkie-talkie since I was a kid. Oh, wait a minute, there was that time in Beirut. As I recall, you were also at the other end of that conversation. If you don't mind, I'm going to sit down and watch the sunrise, seeing how it's too early for the sunbathers. Have you seen the babes on the beach here? They call themselves tourists. It's torture watching them strut around in their bathing suits—a few strings here and there," JJ chuckled. "Next time, can we make it after 5:30 in the morning?"

"Hey, chatty Cathy, if you'll stop thinking about ogling the babes for a minute, we have some serious issues to address."

"Yep, like my finding a job in this little oasis so I can protect your backside. On the other hand, I like presents, even if this radio is a bribe to get me up early. But I digress. Tell me what's going on."

"We may have a chance to wrap up this caper sooner than we thought," Augie said.

"Why is that?" JJ asked, now up off the sand, shoes lying beside his towel as he walked to the water's edge dipping his toes into a receding wave. He pulled back quickly from the icy surf.

"Are you listening to me?" Augie said.

"Yes, I'm listening. I just thought I'd test the water temperature."

"Geez. How did I pull you on this detail? The head guy, the one who thought up this scheme and is trying to make it operational, is expected here in the next few weeks or sooner. He supposedly is bringing some, maybe three, recruits. I've been instructed to train them so they can organize duplicate farms in Detroit, New York, and Tucson. My farm is going to work out of Orlando."

"Interesting. All those cities have huge numbers of travelers going in and out of the country."

"That's right. If the traveler from a country outside of the U.S. comes into the States, then we have a potential to make identities for U.S. recruits to travel to other parts of the world. However, more to the point, if a U.S. citizen is traveling out of the country, they will have a passport in their hand for easy picking. Then we have an identity for an illegal arriving on our doorstep who wants to become another Joe Citizen."

"Any idea what evil deeds these new citizens have up their sleeves?"

"Not yet. But, I'm hoping the head guy will tell me something. After all, I'm thinking he may want the documents to reflect a certain expertise, say, having worked in a nuclear energy plant."

"Ah, then the new citizen can infiltrate one of our plants. That could be nasty," JJ said.

"That's right. By the way, did you find out anything about my roommate Johnny?"

"I did. I dropped in, as a reporter, to the El Paso coroner's office. I told him I was doing a story on illegals crossing the border and wondered if he could tell me if any had landed in his morgue. You know, maybe with some kind of ID, like a Tom, Dick, or Johnny?"

"You didn't say that?" Augie laughed.

"Hey, would I lie to you?"

"You bet you would. What did he say?"

"Honest to God, he told me not a Tom or a Dick, but he did have a Johnny. Johnny Richardson."

"No!" Augie doubled over trying to stifle his laugh, even though the only living thing that would hear him were some sandpipers dashing in and out of the surf. "Was he really dead? Did you get a description?"

"Hold on. Hold on. Yes, I did. From the picture you gave me the coroner's stiff is your Johnny. Definitely dead. Shot at point-blank range through the heart."

"Ooh, bad. He was a pretty nice guy but really didn't fit in. He didn't seem to have a passion for what we were doing. He and Rafi never got along. But still...I guess they mean business. Okay, here's what I want you to do. Tell the director I think we can shut down this operation in a couple of weeks. When I know the actual date Mister Head Guy is going to arrive, I'll alert you so you can prep a SWAT raid. Not only will we get all of this organization for stealing identities, but also falsification of documents and murder. Plus if we strike now, it will set them way back in their timetable because the other farms won't have become operational."

"Are you sure they aren't in place yet?"

"Not from what I've been told so far, but I'll keep digging."

"Does the head guy have a name?"

"Sayid. I haven't had time to perform a search on him, because I had to go shopping for your present. See what you can find out about him from the department. I hope you know that two-way radio gets the local music station. I spared no expense on your gift."

"Thanks a bunch. Now, tell me the good stuff," JJ said. "Is the beautiful Layla still hot for you?"

"Not funny. But, yes. The sad part is that she has me thinking. You know, about how we live...you and I. Do you ever wonder, JJ, about what it would be like to live a *normal* life?"

"Hey, don't go thinking like that."

"JJ, will you do me a favor?"

"Sure, name it."

"Please call my mother. Ask her how she is and is there anything she needs. You can tell her we worked together."

"I'll be happy to call her but don't you think it's time you let her know you're alive?"

"Not yet, but as soon as we finish this assignment, I'm heading to Newburyport. I just want to be sure she's okay. She has a heart problem, and living alone...well, just call her, please."

"I will, but in answer to your previous question, yes, I have thought about quitting. Are you starting to think about her? Catherine? That would not be a good idea."

"To be honest, sometimes when Layla enters the room, I see Catherine—her soft brown eyes...she and I had something very special. At least I thought it was. At the time I began to think about telling the director I was through. After all, you and I have been in the program for how long, at least ten years. I loved her, JJ. God as my witness, I loved her enough to walk away from this...this idealistic notion that I could make a difference in keeping our country safe."

"Hey, there are a lot of women out there."

"No, JJ. There's only one Catherine. I had the good fortune to meet her, but now she's married to another man."

Chapter 8

—•••—

"LUCY, ARE YOU READY?" Catherine called out. "Stephen's in his car seat."

"Just about. I'm zipping up his suitcase now. Go ahead and pull the car out front. My bags are in the foyer. I'll be right down to help you."

Catherine backed out of the garage and drove around the circular driveway to the front door. Scooting out of the car, she popped the trunk of her silver BMW and headed for the front door. Lucy stepped out and handed her Stephen's diaper bag and suitcase. She quickly stepped back inside retrieving her suitcase and carry-on. With everything loaded, Catherine locked the door of her three-story, coral stucco home, pulled out of the driveway and headed west to the Orlando airport.

"Miss Catherine, forgive me for asking, but do you have our passports?"

"No problem, Lucy. Yes, I do. And do you have your driver's license?"

"Yes, and how about Stephen's birth certificate?" Lucy asked.

"We're a three-ring circus aren't we, Lucy?" Catherine said laughing. "This is going to be such fun. Russell said he would meet us at the airport. Yes, I have the birth certificate."

—•••—

An hour-and-a-half later, Catherine pulled into the Park-to-Fly shuttle service. She unloaded the stroller from the trunk of the car.

The shuttle drove up in back of her car and the driver helped put all the bags and the stroller into the van. The sun was beginning to set and the evening air had turned chilly. It would be dark when they boarded the plane for their 8:50 p.m. departure to Miami with a connection to Rio de Janeiro.

The shuttle driver let them off at the departure terminal and took their bags to the outside check-in service. Catherine had printed their boarding passes so checking the bags was quick. She tipped the driver and then tended to Stephen, strapping him in his stroller. She pushed the stroller through the sliding glass doors with Lucy following behind. Stephen's big blue eyes darted from one interesting noise to another, thumb in his mouth, and his favorite teddy bear clutched to his chest.

"Lucy we have plenty of time before our flight boards, do you mind if we stop at that newsstand? I'd like to get a magazine. After we change planes in Miami, I'm hoping Stephen will sleep most of the time during the overnight flight to Brazil."

"No problem, Miss Catherine. With the hustle bustle of getting ready, it's nice to relax. I'll sit over there with Stephen. I see his eyes are growing heavy. He'll probably fall asleep in his stroller. Would you mind picking up a cooking magazine for me while you're there?"

"I'd be glad to. See you in a few minutes."

Lucy settled in her seat with Stephen in his stroller next to her, and closed her eyes to rest. It had been a long hectic day.

—•••—

Layla walked by the newsstand, harvesting. She spotted an infant sleeping in a stroller and the apparent mother had also dozed off. Making a snap decision, Layla softly walked up to the stroller, nudging it. The mother didn't open her eyes, so Layla kept going...faster, adrenalin pumping through her veins. She rounded a bend in the corridor and briskly walked to an open elevator. Punching the button to close the door, she rode down one floor to the departure area. Not missing a step, she strode to the sliding glass doors and out to the waiting van. Opening the hatch, she stooped down to undo the strap and picked up the sleeping child and his diaper bag. She barked at Pasha to put the stroller in the back.

"Hurry up, Pasha, before they see you."

"What the hell do you think you're doing, Layla," Rafi yelled at her from behind the wheel.

"Get going, Rafi," Pasha said slamming his door.

The baby woke up groggy from a deep sleep. Looked around. Not seeing his mother, he began to whimper. "It's all right, little guy, I'm taking care of you while your mommy goes on a trip. Now don't you cry." She dug around his diaper bag and found a bottle of water. Gently sticking the nipple into his mouth, the bottle seemed to quiet him down.

"Layla, I asked you, what the hell do you think you just did?" Rafi snapped under his breath. Merging into traffic, he turned onto the road heading out of the airport.

"Hey, mister high and mighty, a child helps our cover. We'll look like a real family," she hissed back at him.

"Damn, Layla," Rafi growled right back. "They have an Amber Alert system on Route 95. There're cameras all over the airport. They probably have your picture by now. Even our car. Pasha, watch the signs over the highway for the alert. As soon as we see one flash, we'll have to pull off and drive the rest of the way along the ocean. Shit, Layla, I can't believe you jeopardized everything to snatch a kid." Rafi hit the steering wheel several times in exasperation.

Heading out of the airport onto Route 528 toward Cape Canaveral, he restrained himself to keep to the speed limit. The last thing they needed was to be stopped for speeding. Not long after they pulled away from the airport, sirens could be heard heading in the opposite direction.

Chapter 9

— • • • —

THE CHILD FINALLY closed his eyes falling fast asleep. No one spoke as the white van barreled north, traveling a scant five miles per hour over the speed limit. Everyone kept their thoughts to themselves, but tension filled the vehicle as they passed exit after exit. All kept a watchful eye on the electric signs over the highway. No Amber Alert flashed. In just over three hours, Rafi headed over the causeway onto Amelia Island. A few minutes later he pulled the van into the driveway.

"Get that kid a place to sleep," Rafi whispered harshly not wanting to wake the sleeping child. Then meet Pasha and me in the kitchen. Make it snappy. Come on Pasha, we have to do some quick damage control."

It was now close to ten o'clock. Rafi saw the light under Augie's workroom door and barged in. "Augie, we need you. Now! In the kitchen."

"Okay, okay. I'll be right there."

"Augie, I said now!"

Rafi charged into the kitchen, jerked a beer out of the refrigerator, popped the cap and continued his march around the kitchen. Augie joined the two men. Looking from the face of one to the other, he knew in his gut, something bad had happened. He just didn't know what.

"Rafi, are you going to tell me what's wrong or are you just going to keep storming around like a caged animal?" Augie asked.

"Layla did something so stupid, so reckless, I haven't decided whether to kill her or give her a hug," Rafi replied.

"What did she do?" Augie asked, his face now showing alarm as his eyes bore into Rafi.

"She abducted a kid, a little boy, less than two years old. Hell, I don't know how old he is."

"She what?" Augie's gut tightened. His mission just became infinitely more challenging and dangerous. "What the hell prompted her to do that?"

"She said the brat would help our cover. Make us look like a real family," Pasha snarled.

"Where did this happen?" Augie asked.

"The airport," Pasha snapped.

"Thing is," Rafi said, "we have to act fast." Looking at his watch, he said, "It's been about four hours since she nabbed him. There are tons of cameras at the airport which they've probably already checked. They must have every square inch under surveillance." Rafi continued to pace. "Lots of families come and go from Orlando because of Disneyworld, so it will take security some time to comb through all the images. If we're lucky, they won't identify our car right away."

"The State Police must have been alerted by now," Augie said. He took a beer out of the refrigerator and pitched another can to Rafi.

"Ya, we heard sirens just after we left the airport. They could have been called for something else, but we have to assume it was because of the missing baby. We have to get rid of the van. They'll ID it for sure. We have to get rid of it. Pasha, let's wait until morning to ditch it. Turn it in. If you drove over the border into Georgia tonight, the police would spot you for sure. There isn't that much traffic on the road at this hour. But, if you merge into the Jacksonville commuter traffic in the morning, I doubt they'd think twice about another white van, plus the trailer wasn't hooked up at the airport. Augie, you have everything moved out of the trailer?"

"Yes. It's clean as a whistle."

"Okay, if I have to," Pasha said tersely. "Why can't Augie do it?"

"Because, stupid, he has to download the scans we harvested today."

"Oh, uh, right. Smart Augie has to get to work," Pasha snarled.

"Knock it off, Pasha. Yes, return the van to AVIS." Rafi was talking more to himself than the other two. We don't need that big a vehicle now anyway. Then go to another dealer and rent something smaller, maybe an SUV, but not new. Preferably on the silver gray side—lots of those in Florida, and then get your ass back here. We can't use that stroller either. Augie, put it in the attic for now."

"Let's see if there's anything on the news yet," Augie said, clicking the kitchen television remote. The ten o'clock news had just come on. His heart stopped when he saw the woman the reporter was interviewing at the airport, the woman whose baby had just been abducted.

Chapter 10

—•••—

"WELCOME TO CHANNEL 13 news at ten.

An Amber Alert has just been issued for a one-year-old boy, apparently abducted at the Orlando International Airport. Our reporter, Tanya Garcia is there now. Tanya, tell us the latest."

"Yes, Beth, here's what we know so far. Better yet, let the child's mother tell you. Mrs. Hainsworth, what happened to your son?"

Catherine came into the picture, visibly shaken, but appearing to be in control of her emotions. A slight trembling in her hand holding a limp handkerchief gave away how she was really feeling.

"Well, I was at the newsstand. Little Stephen, that's my son's name, was sleeping in his stroller alongside his nanny...over in a waiting area...not far away. When I went to join them, Lucy, that's his nanny, appeared to have nodded off. Stephen was nowhere in sight. I... I... excuse me." Catherine, eyes tearing up, took a deep breath and continued. "I...gave Lucy a nudge...her head jerked up. I asked her where Stephen was. She... she...looked to her side where she had parked his stroller. Then she looked up at me...her eyes filled with horror. We both looked around...in every direction...he was nowhere to be seen."

"What did you do then?" Tanya asked.

"I ran over to a security guard and told him my son was missing, that he must have been kidnapped."

"What did he do?"

"He immediately radioed someone…I don't know who he called, but several airport security guards rushed over to us. I described Stephen…and…and gave them a picture."

"Was it a recent picture, Mrs. Hainsworth?"

"Yes…yes…it was taken several weeks ago, at his birthday party. He turned one."

"Mrs. Hainsworth, please give our listening audience a description of your little boy."

Catherine quickly dabbed the corners of her eyes. "As I said…he's one. He has blonde curls and big blue eyes."

"What was he wearing?"

"It was a night flight, so I put him in his little blue pajamas. There is a little tiger appliqué on the front." This time the tear escaped and ran down her cheek.

"Anything else you can describe?"

"His stroller. They must have left him in his stroller. He was asleep."

"The stroller, what does it look like?" Tanya asked

"It's navy blue with white trim. Please, please, anyone out there, if you see my baby let the police know. And whoever you are who took him, don't hurt him. He's the most precious little human being. Leave him at a church, or… or anywhere. I'm sure you don't mean to harm him. I won't ask any questions. Just please, please don't hurt him." Catherine, tears now streaming down her face, looked straight into the camera and pleaded again with Stephen's abductor not to harm her son.

— • • • —

Rafi and Pasha's eyes were riveted on the small kitchen television set as the news anchor relayed the story of the airport kidnapping. Augie stared at the image of the woman he loved. The only woman he had ever loved. She was in excruciating pain. He also knew, with the timing of the birthday party, that the little boy sleeping upstairs was his son.

Chapter 11

—•••—

LAYLA ENTERED THE KITCHEN. She didn't say anything, waiting for Rafi to speak. She poured herself a glass of wine and sat down at the kitchen table. The three men didn't say a word. They didn't have to. The anger in their eyes coupled with their tight lips said it all. She was in trouble.

"Layla, are you out of your mind? What possessed you to do such a thing?" Augie snapped.

"I don't know. I saw the baby...I thought it was a good idea, to make us look like a family, a family who wants to join the community," she answered so softly they could barely hear her. A tear trickled down her cheek.

"It was stupid...so stupid." Rafi said pounding the table. "Be prepared. Sayid may send you home, back to the family, if they'll have you."

"Oh no, Rafi. They will say I brought disgrace to them. Who knows what they might do to me."

"Well, you should have thought about that before you took the kid," Pasha said, hatred in his eyes.

"Trash the clothes you were wearing along with the kid's," Rafi said sharply. "Augie, get that stroller into the attic and in the morning take Layla to the nearest store where they sell little kids clothes and get what he needs for a few days. Pasha, turn in the damn van as fast as you can. When you get back with another rental car, we'll decide our next move.

"We have to do what the mother asks—drop him off at a church," Augie said, hoping to talk some sense into Layla but knowing it would not work.

"I say, do it now," Pasha said, standing so suddenly that the chair fell over.

Layla also rose from her chair, put her hands on the table, and with squinting eyes leaned forward matching the hatred coming at her. "Now, you men listen to me. Listen to me good. I clean. I cook. I do laundry. I mind the store. I harvest identities. I take your self-righteous shit at being holier-than-thou men. I mean to keep this baby. Do you understand me?" she yelled. Standing up straight, she faced Rafi, her right-hand fingers splayed against his chest, shoving him. "You, Rafi. You suggested a baby would help Augie and me to be a family."

"You're twisting my words, Layla. That is not what I said." Forcefully he removed her hand from his chest and marched to the refrigerator for another beer.

She stomped after her brother, stabbing him in the chest again with her finger. "Oh, yes. Oh, yes it is," she screamed at him. "And if any one of you tries to take this baby from me," she hissed, "I will take him away. We will leave and you can fend for yourselves."

—•••—

Augie left them, still shouting at each other. He went to Layla's room where she had made a bed of pillows on the floor for Stephen. He tiptoed over to the sleeping baby and sat down crossed-legged beside him. He peered with wonder at the beautiful child with golden curls, his little mouth open, slightly bowed, breathing rhythmically in sleep. He reached over and lightly touched the soft baby skin of his chubby arm. Stephen opened his eyes and looked at Augie. There was no fear. Instead, he raised his arms, asking to be picked up. Augie did as he was asked, lifting the infant, cradling him to his body, his chin moving slowly over the golden curls.

"My little Stephen, I will protect you. No harm will come to you I swear. I promise you and I will be back with your mother as soon as we can," Augie whispered. The door opened slightly, a band of light falling on the scarred wooden floor illuminating Augie holding the baby.

"You like him, yes?" Layla whispered. She had left her hysterics in the kitchen. "He likes you, Augie. Look. He's not even crying."

"Shh. He's fallen asleep," Augie replied softly, as he laid the baby back down on the pillows.

"Oh, Augie, this will work," she said kneeling in back of him, her arms around his shoulders. "You'll see. I'll be a wonderful mother," she whispered twisting around, looking into his eyes, placing her lips on his.

Chapter 12

— • • • —

CATHERINE PACED IN a private room in the American Airlines' hospitality suite where airport security had escorted her and Lucy. It was now midnight. She looked out the window seeing only her reflection in the night glass, her tears abating for the moment.

Chief Ortega, Orlando Police Department, arrived on the scene directing a team of officers to sweep Terminals A and B, as well as the parking garages. All airline security gates were alerted to be on the lookout for a person acting suspiciously and pushing a little boy in a stroller. If they spotted anything out of the ordinary, they were to report the sighting immediately to airport security, the nearest police officer or call the police department. An officer would be dispatched to check the passenger's identification. Of course, there were hundreds of women and men pushing strollers, and with confusion always a part of traveling, everyone looked under duress.

Catherine turned abruptly from the window, hugging herself where she wanted her son to be, in her arms. Lucy began sobbing uncontrollably. Catherine knelt in front of her. She gently shook the nanny's shoulders so she had to look into Catherine's red eyes.

"Lucy. Lucy, stop it. Pull yourself together. I need you now more than ever." Her eyes pleaded with the distraught woman.

"Oh, Miss Catherine, what have I done?"

Catherine gathered the overwrought woman in her arms holding her tight. She moved to sit beside her on the couch still holding her, rocking back and forth.

"Lucy," she whispered, "if some deranged person wants to take a baby, they will find a way to do so. Come on now. Please, stop crying. The police will be back soon to ask you again what you saw. You have to pull yourself together."

The door to the suite burst open. Manny led the way with Brenda and Fred on his heels.

"Oh, Manny," Catherine said, walking swiftly to him and sinking into his protective arms, "I'm so glad you're here." She turned to Fred who hugged her as well.

Brenda stepped in and held her friend in a tight embrace. She whispered in Catherine's ear, "We're going to find Stephen." Brenda then sat beside Lucy and put her arms around the red-eyed woman, whose face was streaked with rivers of tears. "He'll be found. You'll see," she whispered, holding her tight.

"How did you know we were here?" Catherine asked looking from one to the other, dabbing her eyes.

"The chief called me when he saw you were from my jurisdiction," Manny said. "Of course, he didn't know that we knew each other. I called Fred, filled him in on what little I knew, and he said he wanted to go to the airport with me. Naturally, Brenda joined us."

The door to the suite swung open again. Chief Ortega hustled up to the group. A portly man, he was out of breath from scurrying around to check with his officers.

"Any news, Chief?" Catherine asked.

"Nothing as yet, Mrs. Hainsworth."

Catherine introduced her friends to the chief. He had already met Lucy, who was still huddled on the couch.

"We've completed the initial sweep, and the teams are now retracing their steps—searching all cleaning closets, luggage areas, and restrooms—opening all doors. I just finished talking to the cruisers. Of course, they're on the lookout for the boy—they have his picture. We don't have anything else to go on. Let me change that. We're getting lots of calls about babies in a stroller, and we're trying to check them out as fast as they come in."

"What about surveillance cameras?" Manny asked.

"We have an officer talking to the airport security people to pinpoint the area and the time frame the baby was taken," the chief said. "No word as yet as to what they've found. It's as if he vanished into thin air. But don't you worry, Mrs. Hainsworth. We won't stop until we find him. I suggest you go home. I'll call you in a few hours to let you know how we're doing. There's nothing else you can do here."

"There must be something I can do to help. Please, there must be something," Catherine pleaded.

"There is one thing that will help is to keep your story in front of the cameras. I'm sure they will be camped out at your house. Tell them you suggest they go home—that you'll hold a press briefing at ten in the morning. That way, maybe they'll leave and give you a little peace. I'll call you by nine o'clock with an update, so you'll have something to say, if nothing more than to please keep a lookout for your little boy. I suggest you have a couple of different pictures ready to show them. Wherever the person took him, there's a chance somebody will recognize the little tyke."

"All right. I guess that makes sense," Catherine said, her body slumping.

"Cat, I'll take you and Lucy home," Manny offered. "Where's your car?"

"I left it at Park-To-Fly, about a mile from the airport."

"I know where it is. Come on everyone. Fred, I'll drop you and Brenda off at Cat's car so you can drive it to her house. We'll meet up with you there."

—•••—

Manny pulled into Catherine's driveway, navigating around two television network vans. Flashbulbs punctuated the crisp night air, as Catherine and Lucy slid out of the backseat of the squad car. Brenda and Fred pulled up in back of Manny and joined them.

Catherine stood with Manny on the brick steps leading to her front door. The media instantly pushed their microphones within a foot of their faces.

"There's nothing more to report tonight, folks," Manny said. "Ms. Hainsworth has a brief statement, and then I suggest you all go home and get some rest."

Manny turned to Catherine, giving her a nod to go ahead.

"Thank you for being here. I need your help. It's of the utmost importance to keep this story in front of everyone in range of your signals. As Captain Salinas said, there is nothing more to report tonight. The Orlando police are continuing to search the airport, and the Amber Alert has been triggered. I'll give you an update tomorrow. I guess...it's really today," she said looking at her watch. "Nearly three o'clock. Anyway, there will be an update at ten this morning. Until then I have nothing further to say."

Catherine turned and put the key in the front door lock. Hesitating, she quickly turned to face the reporters. "Naturally, if we find my son, you will all be alerted immediately." Suddenly tears sprang from her eyes. "Let me say, once again, you...who took my son, please don't hurt him. Please take him to a church. Let him go."

—•••—

Augie leaned forward switching off the television. His heart was breaking, but his brain was trying desperately to come up with a way to return his baby, and himself, to Catherine. Drawn again to look at his son, he crept up the stairs to Layla's room and quietly pushed open the door. Layla was sleeping on the bed, and little Stephen was still where Augie had left him—on the pillows. He knelt beside the boy, taking in the miracle that lay before him. He carefully leaned over and kissed him softly on his chubby cheek. Stephen opened his eyes part way, smiled, then stuck his thumb in his mouth and went back to sleep.

Chapter 13

—•••—

AUGIE LAID ON the futon in his workroom, staring at the ceiling. The room was small but not cramped. He liked to have a place where he could take a quick nap between the long bouts hunched over the computer. Several solutions began to emerge in his head. Sayid would be coming with three recruits sometime in the next two weeks. Maybe he could wrap-up the mission and return little Stephen to Catherine. Hopefully, she would accept him back into her life as well. But right now he couldn't think about Catherine and the pain he saw in her eyes at the news conference last night. No! The best thing for him to do right now was to concentrate on fulfilling the mission without anyone getting hurt or, worse, killed.

First, he had to alert JJ to the new situation. He reached for his cell but stopped when he heard Stephen crying in Layla's bedroom. Augie raced upstairs and pushed the door open. The tot was sitting on his makeshift bed, tears rolling down his fat little pink cheeks, his mouth quivering. "Mommy, Mommy."

"Hey, hey, little man, it's okay. Augie's here," he said, lifting the baby into his arms, wrapping the blanket around him.

Layla rolled over under her covers and looked at Augie with the child. "Augie, you like him, yes?"

"Layla, it was a stupid thing you did," he snapped. "I'll take him downstairs. See what we have that he can eat."

"Augie, he likes you," she said ignoring his sharp tongue. "See how he stopped crying, laying his head on your chest, sucking his thumb. I know you'll thank me for bringing him to you. Thank me, so maybe we can be a family."

"Layla, you're living in a fantasy world. I suggest you get up and make a list of what the little guy needs."

"Did Pasha leave with the van?"

"Yes. He called a little bit ago. He thinks he can make it back here in about an hour. You can take the new car and do some shopping."

Augie headed down to the kitchen hugging the little boy to his body. It was a wonderful feeling—holding this little one, holding his son. *Catherine, be brave,* he thought. *I promise nothing will happen to our boy. I'll keep him safe and return him to your arms soon, my love.*

In the kitchen, he found a box of crackers and a banana. "This will have to do for now, Stephen." Augie sat the boy down on a couple of pillows he found in the living room, so he could eat off the table. Quickly changing his mind, fearing the baby would fall, he sat down with him on his lap, breaking the crackers into smaller pieces, and cutting up the banana. "Now, we have to do something about those curls young man." Augie pulled out his cell and took a picture of the tot smiling up at him, the curls circling his head.

Setting him on the floor, Augie searched through the cabinet drawers and finally found a pair of scissors. "Now, my man, you are going to get a haircut so you won't be so recognizable from your television picture. From the looks of this golden mop on your head, I doubt you've ever had one. I've had to do this a few times on myself so let's see what we can do for you."

Augie sat on the floor with Stephen braced between his legs for support. The child sat very still, eating his banana as his curls started piling up on the floor around him. Snipping off the last curl, Augie folded it in a paper napkin and stuffed it in his pocket. Then he stood Stephen up and slowly turned him around, tilting his head from one side to the other. "Not a bad job, mister, if I do say so myself."

The back screen door slammed shut and Pasha entered the kitchen. "Holy shit. Look at him, will you?" Pasha said throwing a set of car keys onto the kitchen table.

Stephen began to cry. "Watch your mouth when you're with this little guy, Pasha," Augie admonished.

Before Pasha could answer, Layla hollered from upstairs. "Somebody come help me down with this the baby stuff I found in the attic."

"Pasha, you go help her, while I clean up this mess from his hair cut."

"Shit. That kid is nothing but trouble. Shut up, Layla, I'm coming," Pasha yelled back at her.

— • • • —

Augie put on a fresh pot of coffee. Layla was in her room putting Stephen down for a nap in the crib she found in the attic. Rafi and Pasha were eating cereal at the kitchen table when Layla came down to join the group rubbing her arms. "It's cold. I'm going to have to get some warmer clothes."

They all had pulled on their jeans as well as long-sleeved pullovers. "Stop complaining, Layla. You were snug in your bed while I was out this morning when it was really cold. The weather station said that forty-eight degrees at night was below normal for this time of year. Don't be a sissy," Pasha said, scowling again at her.

"Okay, let's go over what we're going to do here with that kid, plus I had a conversation with Sayid earlier," Rafi said. "I told Sayid what you did, Layla. Right away he was all for sending you on the first plane back to Pakistan, but after I told him why you did it, to add credence to our cover story, he began to warm to the idea. If things go well when he visits us, you'll probably be forgiven."

"I say, we take him to a church in Jacksonville, and leave him with a note pinned to his shirt," Augie said pulling a chair out from under the table. Turning it around, he sat straddling the seat.

"Didn't you hear me last night? Don't go there, Augie," Layla flared with an icy stare back at him.

"Well, we may still have to do that, but right now let's see what happens in the next few days," Rafi said. "With the haircut you gave the kid, Augie, I doubt anyone will recognize him. Layla be sure you always keep a hat on him when you go out. What baby stuff did you find in the attic?"

"Oh, my, it was loaded," she said sweetly. "The crib you already know about, and, Augie, there's a highchair, if you'll get it, and a beat up stroller. All the basics—good enough for starters."

"So, then all the brat needs is some food and clothes?" Pasha asked.

"Pasha, stop calling him a brat. His name is Stephen. Honestly, you can be so...so, mean," Layla said. "And, yes, you're right, he just needs a few clothes, bedding to fit the crib, and, of course some diapers. That reminds me, I'd better get going before he wakes up. Augie, if you hear Stephen, will you tend to him? He seems to be quiet when he's around you. I put the last diaper on him when I changed him for his nap. On the other hand, I'll take him with me. I don't trust you three...I wonder when we should start potty training?"

"Good Lord. This is getting way out of hand," Pasha said, slamming his coffee cup down, spilling the remains on the table.

"Calm down, Pasha," Rafi said. "Tell me about the van."

"I didn't have a problem leaving here at 6:30 this morning like you suggested. You were right, Rafi, the traffic was thick. I drove about an hour into Georgia where I spotted a car dealer who also offered rentals. He had just pulled in his dealership with a Dunkin coffee and doughnut. I told him I didn't need the large van anymore or the trailer. He unlocked the door and told me to look around while he drank his coffee. He didn't have shit, so I ended up renting a smaller Ford SUV down the street at a place he suggested. But the car still seats seven."

"I told you not to rent a car at the same place you turned in the van. Now, if the police locate the dealer, he can tip them off about the new rental. Shit, do I have to do everything?"

"Ya, well, he was the only one open. You aren't listening to me, Rafi. I didn't rent from him but from his buddy down the street. I had to wait a half an hour for him to get his body into work. And just how was I going to get to another lot further away to rent a car? Huh? Huh? Answer me that."

"Okay, I see your point. Tomorrow you can drop me off at a dealer in Jacksonville. I'll buy a car and pick you up down the road after you turn this one in. Shit, this is a three-ring circus. Between you and Layla—"

"Don't you ever compare me to her," Pasha said, looking steely eyed at Rafi.

"Stop! Calm down, everyone," Augie said. "What did Sayid have to say, Rafi? Did he give you a date, a time he'd be here? Where does he want to stay, and are the three recruits he mentioned coming with him?"

"Well, listen to you with all the questions," Rafi said, refreshing his coffee from the pot on the counter.

"And lots of questions at that!" Augie snapped. "Don't forget it's my neck on the line to have new documents finished, ready to show them how the whole production process works."

"They'll be here Thursday, a week from today, and yes, he's bringing the three men."

Layla returned to the kitchen holding Stephen and grabbed the keys off the table.

"Layla, I want you to make reservations at the Florida Inn, four rooms, and two nights for Sayid and his men. They're flying into Jacksonville and expect to be here by dinner. I also don't want you to eat with us or even come to the inn. Sayid was never happy that I let you join me. He doesn't want women on the farms. He thinks they're nothing but trouble. Which, of course, this kid you're holding, the product of your little stunt, proves his point."

"Criticize me. Blame me for every little mishap. That's all you do. Well, stop it! You can expect me back in an hour, or maybe never." She snatched her empty coffee cup off the table with her free hand, deposited it in the sink, and stormed out of the kitchen.

The three men kept their mouths shut. Augie hit the remote turning on the TV. The news channel was still selected from the night before. The screen filled with Catherine's image telling the reporters that there was nothing new to report. No sightings. She again pleaded for information and asked his abductor not to harm her son. He snapped the remote again removing her from the screen. His gut twisted. He excused himself and went out for his morning run.

Chapter 14

—•••—

"HELLO. MAY I SPEAK to Meri Hutchinson?" JJ asked, tapping his pen on the piece of paper with her telephone number.

"Who's calling?" the woman asked in a friendly voice.

"An acquaintance. I knew her son, Stephen. In fact, we worked closely together for many years. He talked about his mother often—I felt I knew her. My name is Jerry Johnstone."

"I'm sorry, sir, but Mrs. Hutchinson passed away about six months ago."

"Oh...oh, I see. Then who are you?"

"I was Mrs. Hutchinson's nurse. She was a wonderful woman."

"Yes, she was. You sound like you were fond of her."

"Oh, yes. We became good friends for the few short months I took care of her. She insisted I live with her because I didn't have any family. And then, just before she died, she made arrangements so that I could remain in the house for as long as I liked. She even left me the money to take care of the house."

"Did she...did she suffer?"

"Not really. She went to sleep one night looking at the pictures of her son and grandson on the nightstand by her bed. As was her custom, she would kiss her fingers and then touch the images in the two pictures. She closed her eyes and never woke up."

"What is her grandson's name?"

"Stephen. She was so happy when his mother named him after his father. He died, too. It's been over a year now since he passed. But I guess you know that."

"Yes, I was with him. Did she tell you the name of Stephen's mother?"

"Oh, yes. A lovely woman. She wrote to Meri often. Her name is Catherine."

Chapter 15

—•••—

THREE CUSTOMERS SAT at the bar, as well as two tables of tourists who had stopped in for an early afternoon drink. The Palace Saloon was the oldest bar in Florida. The swinging saloon doors with clear leaded-glass windows were flanked on the left side by a larger-than-life statue of a bearded pirate. A red knife strap cut across his slate-blue jacket. Tan pants covered his right leg and were bound at the top of his peg leg.

Augie pushed through the swinging doors and took a seat at the far end of the old wooden bar. Mirrors spanned the back of the bar reflecting three life-size paintings between the windows on the opposite wall. The paintings depicted gentlemen in early American times sitting at tables in front of the window. The gentlemen were dressed in red waistcoats, ruffled shirts peeking out at the neckline and extending from the jacket cuffs. Light tan leggings were tucked into black shiny boots. The men posing for the pictures were long gone, but their portraits remained in the cozy atmosphere where they probably spent many enjoyable hours.

"What can I get you, mister?" JJ asked. Both men locked on to the eyes of the other.

"I'll have a Bloody Mary, please, with extra salt on the rim," Augie said with a friendly smile.

"That's our specialty. One Bloody Mary with extra salt coming right up," JJ replied affably.

JJ brought Augie his drink and then leaned against the gleaming bar polished to a glass finish from patrons over the years leaning on their elbows, holding their drinks. With his forearm resting on the bar, JJ turned slightly so he faced the kitchen, away from the tables and anyone sitting on the high-back barstools. Augie turned toward the kitchen as well, putting his feet up on the rung of the empty barstool next to him. Nobody could see they were in deep conversation. Every couple of minutes one or the other would laugh at a nonexistent joke. A couple of times JJ went to refresh a customer's drink or to take the order of a tourist who sauntered in.

"I think we have a chance to break the ring next Thursday," Augie said quietly. "The big guy is coming to visit with three new recruits. They're supposed to set up operations like we have here and Rafi said I'm to train them. They're arriving Thursday, late afternoon, supposedly by dinnertime. Layla is making reservations for them at the Florida Inn on Fourth Street, and the men are scheduled to have dinner together at the inn. Get your team in place, but only set up surveillance on Thursday. I want to be sure everyone shows up. Layla will not be with us, so you'll have to grab her at the house. Seems the top guy doesn't like to do business with women. I'll take pictures with my cell phone as soon as I get a chance, and send them to you."

JJ laughed, giving Augie a friendly jab on the arm, and went to take an order from a couple who had just taken seats at the other end of the bar. He returned to Augie taking up his stance facing the kitchen.

"Did you see Catherine on the news last night?" Augie asked.

"Yes, and again this morning," JJ said. "I can't imagine a sicko pulling such a thing."

"It was Layla."

JJ looked full into Augie's tortured face. Other than his turning to face Augie, there was no hint from the demeanor of either man telegraphing the magnitude of the words that lay in the silence between them.

"Naturally, when you get Layla, you have to take care that little Stephen doesn't get hurt."

"Naturally."

"JJ, the reporters refer to Catherine as Mrs. Hainsworth. She named the boy Stephen. He's one. She said he had a birthday party a few weeks ago, which would put it late January. The night I spent with Catherine, before going to New York when the operation ended with my being shot, is almost nine months to the day he was born. JJ, I know he's my son. Forget what I said in the hospital. Forget everything I said about her. Seeing the pain in her eyes...tore at my gut. I can't block my feelings for her any longer. I have to return to her. I want to raise Stephen with her. JJ, you've got to help me." Augie looked beseechingly at his friend.

"Well, partner, I also have news. I called your mother this morning, as you requested. A lady answered. She asked who I was, and I gave her my name and that I had worked with Mrs. Hutchinson's son."

Augie stared into JJ's eyes. He saw that bad news was coming. "Was it my mother?"

"No. The woman said she was Mrs. Hutchinson's nurse. Augie, your mother passed away six months ago. I'm sorry. We were too late."

Augie dropped his head down, staring into the bottom of his empty glass.

JJ took the glass from his friend's limp fingers. "I'm sorry," he whispered. Giving Augie some time to absorb the bad news, JJ waited on three new customers, returned to the back of the bar, made another stiff Bloody Mary, and set it in front of Augie.

Augie straightened up on the barstool, taking a long swallow of his drink. His eyes were now slits filled with steely determination. "JJ, we have a potential problem with Catherine in the picture, actually, several. I have no doubt that Manny is heading up the search for Stephen. Also, Catherine is not one to sit idly by without bringing the full force of her assets to bear on finding her son. The longer it takes for us to arrest these terrorist farmers," Augie spit out, "the greater the likelihood that the mission will be compromised. Manny will not stop until he finds her son."

"I hear ya."

"Kidnapping is one of those crimes where officials have to keep the story going—pictures of the person abducted, in this case a toddler, plastered all over the newspapers, running non-stop on the television networks."

"Those big blue eyes and blonde curls wrench your heart out," JJ said.

"The curls are gone, except for one." Hutch reached in his pocket and withdrew the paper napkin. He carefully unfolded the napkin and touched the blonde curl. "I cut them off this morning," he said folding and returning the napkin to his pocket. "Rafi told Layla to keep a hat on his head if she takes him out. I'm trying to get Layla to take him to a church, like Catherine requested. But she has some cockamamie idea that, with a baby, we look like a family. Then there's the top guy, Sayid, the one coming on Thursday. He doesn't trust women. It's a powder keg. Rafi told Layla to stay in the house and away from Sayid. Everyone, except Pasha, is warming to the idea of keeping the baby around. Rafi even said that maybe it wasn't such a bad idea after all. Shit, if they harm one hair on his little head, I swear I'll kill every one of them—on the spot."

Chapter 16

—•••—

DAY THREE! The reporters, some with their television vans, camped out again on Catherine's street. She told them there would be an update at three o'clock. As promised Catherine stepped out of her house into the warm sunshine at precisely three. The warmth of the sun didn't seem to register as she pulled her black sweater tight around her shoulders knotting it in front over her white silk blouse. She had nothing new to report, but again pleaded to the kidnapper to take her son to a church, but, above all else, not to harm him.

"I have another picture for you taken at Stephen's birthday party. I'd appreciate your showing it on your next broadcast. The police have scheduled a meeting with me and Stephen's nanny this afternoon, and I anticipate I will have something more to tell you after meeting with them, perhaps as soon as this evening. Thank you again for your assistance." She set a time for the evening update in order to air on the ten o'clock news.

Manny had called earlier to tell her he received the airport's surveillance pictures. He thought it would be a good idea if she and Lucy came to the department to take a look at the video clips. Maybe they would spot something that his team had missed.

—•••—

Immediately after the press conference Catherine and Lucy left for the police station. The sergeant at the desk asked them to take a seat. Someone would be down shortly to escort them to the conference room. They didn't have to wait long. They had no more than taken a seat on a bench when Manny came hustling down the stairs. He gave her a brief hug, nodding to Lucy. He then asked the ladies to follow him to the conference room.

Sergeant Dani Trotter, Manny's research and technical support team member, was setting up the equipment on the large oak conference table and greeted them as they entered. "Hi, Mrs. Hainsworth. I can't imagine how unbelievably hard this is for you."

"Dani, please call me Catherine. I'd like you to meet Lucy Sullivan. Lucy is Stephen's nanny and was with us when it happened."

Lucy sat down, shrinking into the hard oak chair, trying to disappear.

Fred and George, Manny's two detectives, entered the room with several computer discs in hand. Fred rounded the table to Catherine, giving her a quick hug. "Brenda sends her love. I guess you told her you'd stop by your office when you finished here."

"Yes, I did, but I may take Lucy home first."

Dani loaded the discs into the two laptops. Each laptop was connected to a projector, which beamed the images onto two eight-foot screens mounted side-by-side on the far wall. The shades were drawn over three large windows in an attempt to darken the room.

"There's a directory on each disc," Dani said. "The video file names are pretty much self-explanatory, as you can see, the third-floor shop area, baggage-claim-terminal-A, ticket-counter terminal-A, etcetera."

"We're going to start with the abduction. This will be hard for you to watch, especially you, Lucy. Remember, what we're trying to find are clues. Something that will give us a lead. Are you ready?" Manny asked, looking at Lucy and then Catherine.

"Yes, Captain, I'm ready," Lucy replied. She wiggled to sit up straighter, looked more alert—maybe because she felt she could finally be of some help. Catherine stared straight ahead at the blank screens.

Dani started the video. "Note the date and timestamp in the top right corner—February 16, 6:15 p.m.," Dani said.

"Catherine, Lucy, the second you see something tell us, and we'll freeze the frame," Manny said.

The video ran for a few seconds when a woman, with a large straw hat, entered the picture from the right side. She walked slowly by where Lucy sat with Stephen in his stroller. Lucy's chin was down, almost resting on her chest. It was obvious she had dozed off. The straw hat turned and again walked to where Lucy was dozing, but this time she didn't pass. She slowly stepped up to the stroller and moved it slightly.

"Oh, no," Lucy cried out, immediately putting her hand over her mouth, as she tried to stifle any further sound. Her face became contorted as she witnessed what was happening in the video. Catherine sat perfectly straight but her face gave away the emotions coursing through her body. Her eyes widened in fear at the same time her hands clutched the arms of the chair. She held back the tears.

"Look, there she goes," Dani said. "The straw-hat woman is pushing the stroller away. She's walking very fast now."

"She's heading for that bank of elevators," Fred said.

Everyone leaned forward, straining to catch every detail of the action being projected onto the screen. The woman with the stroller scooted in and around other passengers pulling carry-on bags—some talking to each other, some walking quickly as if trying not to miss their flight.

"She's pushing Stephen into the elevator," Catherine said. "She must have hit the button to close the door—it slid closed so quickly."

"The down arrow over the door lit up," Manny said, abruptly standing up, an impulsive reaction as if he could see better. Patting is left breast pocket, he absentmindedly drew out a piece of Nicorette gum, unwrapped it, popping it in his mouth. "Look it stopped and the arrow turned to a three. That's Level 3, the ticket counter and departure area. Dani, check the file directory of the second disc for Level 3."

"Let's try this one," Dani said. "It's the departure and ticket counter, Terminal A."

The screen on the right filled with the video.

"I don't see the elevators," Fred said. "Dani, try another one."

"Okay. Here we go. This disc is labeled Elevators-center-ticket-counter."

"Now go to 6:15 p.m. That's just a minute or two before we saw the straw hat," Manny said.

The video progressed to 6:18 p.m.

"There," Manny said. "Dani, freeze it. The straw hat is leaving the elevator. God, look at the crowd."

"Heck with the crowd," Fred said. "Look at all the strollers."

"And straw hats," Lucy whispered.

"There, there, going thru the sliding glass doors. Isn't that her? The straw hat. Black slacks. White blouse...I think," Catherine said. She was now standing beside Manny, not able to tie herself to the chair. She walked around the corner of the table, pointing at the spot on the screen. "Look, a man ran up. The straw hat, the woman is lifting a small child...it's Stephen. I know it is. I can see his curls." She exhaled a small gasp, raising her hand to her throat.

"She's getting into the back seat. The man is shoving the stroller into the back of the van. He slammed the doors shut," Dani said. Now, she too was on her feet.

"Freeze it, Dani. Freeze it," Manny yelled. "Blow it up. Can we get that license plate?"

"Manny, it's at an angle," Fred said. "Everything on the plate is blurred together."

"Wait," Catherine said, almost screaming. "The plate. Is that a graphic of Texas?"

"You could be right, Catherine," Dani said. "Let me copy this frame. I'll take it to my lab computer where I can enhance it."

"Now we have something to put out on the wire," Manny said. "White van, looks like a Ford van with a Texas license plate. Dani, when you blow up the frame, see if you can pinpoint the year and exact model of the van."

Catherine looked away from the screen. "I told the press there might be more information this evening. Dani, please call with what you find. The Amber Alert is only active for five days and then the child is removed from the ticker. But, if there's new information, it can be extended."

Catherine closed her eyes whispering a prayer. "Please, dear God, keep him safe...Stephen, we're coming."

Chapter 17

—•••—

"GOOD EVENING FROM Channel 13. It's ten o'clock and time for the top of the news.

We have an update on the story we've been following for you—the abduction of the one-year-old boy, Stephen Hainsworth. Police report the van thought to be involved in the case is a white Ford, minivan—model 2009 E-150 XL. The license tag was partially obstructed, but it appears to be a Texas plate.

The Amber Alert is still in force. Please take another look at this adorable little boy. If you see him, or the vehicle shown here, please call the number at the bottom of your screen.

Now for other news in our area."

Chapter 18

—•••—

NOTHING WENT AS planned. Sayid arrived at the house instead of the Florida Inn at one o'clock instead of five. He had flown his own plane to Amelia Island instead of taking a commercial flight to Jacksonville. A rental car was waiting at the small airstrip. He brought no one with him. There would be no dinner at the Florida Inn.

Layla quickly improvised the scheduled dinner plans. The inn offered to prepare an Italian meal, which could easily be transferred from the containers directly to large platters and served family style. The food would be ready for pick up in an hour. Already nervous about being in the same house as Sayid, she didn't dare ask Augie to watch Stephen. She would have to manage the baby and pick up the cartons at the same time.

With the air still warm from the afternoon sun, the four men sat congenially in the backyard under a large oak tree dripping with Spanish moss. Congenially, but Augie's mind was going at warp speed. Should he call off the SWAT raid? Sayid's arriving alone—what did it mean? No one had been recruited as yet? If that was true, then shutting down the farm now made sense. The raid should go ahead as planned.

Sayid finally broke into the chitchat and addressed the business at hand. "Augie, I would like you to give me a detailed briefing—how you produce the documents from the point you download the scans."

"No problem, but Rafi said that you were bringing two or three others with you."

"I changed my mind," Sayid replied pointedly.

"Do you want me to start after dinner, or wait until tomorrow?" Augie asked.

"Let's start now. I won't be staying over. That's why I arrived a little early. I plan to fly out of here by midnight."

"How come so quick?" Augie asked. "We have a lot of information to cover."

"Let's just say, one can't be too careful where one is seen."

"Pasha, why don't you get our friend something to drink," Rafi said. "A beer, Sayid, or something stronger?"

"A cup of coffee will do nicely. I must stay alert. Now, Augie, please begin."

"Give me a minute to turn the equipment on, so it'll be ready for a demonstration," Augie replied. He left the men in the garden while Pasha headed into the kitchen to fix the coffee. Augie went to his workroom, closed the door, fished out his cell, and punched JJ's code.

"What's up?"

"Major change in plans. Sayid is here now. We're staying at the house. Everything is to be discussed over the next four or so hours. Be ready but watch out for Layla. She's picking up our dinners and has Stephen with her. As far as I can tell, Sayid is packing a gun. Rafi and Pasha as well. Sayid came alone. You scouted out the back gate, front and back door. I'll make sure we go into the kitchen. Again, Layla will be upstairs with Stephen. She has a gun in her nightstand. My guess is you can start the sweep around midnight—maybe a little before. I'll turn the back porch light on as a signal to enter. Wait for it."

Pasha brought out a carafe of fresh coffee that Layla had thought to leave on the kitchen counter. "Layla should be back any minute," Rafi said. "If it's all right with you, Sayid, let's have a bite to eat first while the food is hot. Augie can give you a summary over dinner, and then show you the specifics."

Layla honked the horn once, indicating she needed help with the food. Augie and Pasha went out to the car. Augie, unbuckling

Stephen, lifted him out of his car seat. As Pasha and Layla brought the containers into the kitchen, Rafi and Sayid came in from the garden.

"Let's eat in the kitchen," Pasha said. "I'm tired of being bitten by those damn no-see-em flies. Besides, it's cooling off."

Layla transferred the food from the containers to the serving plates, while Pasha set the table. Augie put Stephen in his highchair and broke up some crackers onto the tray. The little guy looked from one man to the other as they chitchatted about the weather and Sayid's flight down from Detroit. Once dinner was on the table, Layla fed Stephen some baby food—peas and applesauce. Someone dropping in would have thought it was a loving family having dinner together—not a group of farmers bent on aiding illegals, terrorists really, into the country whose aim was to destroy the American way of life forever.

Layla didn't like to be in the same room with Sayid. Stephen, however, seemed to find the men's conversation fascinating. Eating spoonful after spoonful of pureed food that Layla served him, his eyes continually darted to whoever spoke next. Layla made sure the men had what they needed, and then left with Stephen.

"Well, the boy seems to be well behaved," Sayid said. "Rafi, let him stay a few more weeks. If your household settles in, then go ahead and keep the boy. If not, well, you know what to do. Under no circumstance is this project to be compromised. By anybody! Certainly not a baby."

—•••—

The ensuing hours were spent huddled by the computer. Augie had produced a set of documents for Sayid, with detailed instructions on the equipment needed—ink, paper, cutting and laminating equipment. At eleven thirty, Sayid stood up and backed away from the computer.

"That about covers it," Augie said. "How about we go in the kitchen for a fresh cup of coffee before you take off?"

Everyone stretched, ambling out of the cramped workroom to the kitchen. Each helped himself to coffee and spread out around the table.

It was a dark night but relatively mild temperatures for late February. Clouds covered the moon and the stars. No one in the houses on the street would have noticed a black van, without headlights, slowly drive up and stop two houses away from the little print shop.

"How many documents will you require over the next month, or so?" Augie asked as he walked over to the coffeepot on the counter next to the back door.

"About a hundred to start with...preferably from different areas of the country. That's why we must establish more farms. I like how you organized the process, Augie," Sayid said. "Rafi, I will be back in three days with Masud. I want him to see the operation. He's the one who thought we should establish the document preparation in three or four parts of the United States—giving us a wider range of identities from various locations. When I give him the report Augie prepared and tell him how Augie has organized the process, I think he will want to setup centers in several European countries, as well as Canada and maybe even Australia. Nine-eleven will look tame when he has everyone in place, triggering several plots at once. Only this time, documented citizens living in each country will just melt into the background. No last minute border crossings."

"Excuse me," Augie said. "I have to turn the equipment off. I'll be right back. Do you want more coffee anyone?"

"Yes, please," Sayid said. "I can't have a foggy head on my trip back to Detroit."

"Pasha, can you make another pot while I turn off the computer and printers?" Augie asked. He didn't wait for a reply.

Augie strolled down the hall, turned on the bathroom light, closed the door behind him, flushed the toilet, and turned the tap on full. He fished out his phone and punched JJ's code.

"Hello."

"Abort. Abort."

"Roger."

"There's a bigger fish coming in three days. Sayid is leaving shortly. Get a picture of him if you can with your night equipment. I'll call you in the morning."

—•••—

Eight black-suited men stealthily returned to their black van, silently climbing inside. The vehicle's doors closed with a soft click of the latch. Sixteen minutes later JJ snapped a picture out of the rear, one-way glass window. After Sayid's car turned the corner, the black van inched away from the curb vanishing into the night.

Chapter 19

— • • • —

MANNY AND HIS team were stymied. All they had was a white van with perhaps a Texas license plate, and a woman wearing a big straw hat, white blouse, and dark slacks. Dani sent out an APB with these few pieces of information, but so far no one had called in with a sighting. The Amber Alert was due to expire in two days unless they came up with some leads.

Manny's black Labrador, Peaches, was sleeping fitfully on her pillow, looked up startled, when Manny's phone rang. The desk sergeant said she was transferring a call from a man. He said he owned a car rental company in Georgia. The caller wanted to speak to the person handling the child abduction case at the Orlando Airport.

"For Pete's sake, put him through," Manny snapped. He nervously tapped his pen on the blank pad in front him, waiting for the caller to be connected.

"Hello, Captain Salinas?" the caller asked.

"Yes, yes, I'm Captain Salinas. I understand you're calling about the white van. Do you think you've seen it?"

"I believe so. In fact, we just washed it down so we can put it out in the lot. I saw the Texas plate and thought I'd give you a call. It came in with a trailer."

"Who returned it and do you have a number of the rental agency in Texas?"

"Hang on a minute. Let me get the paperwork."

"George, we may finally have something," Manny said, putting his hand over the receiver's mouthpiece. Get Dani in here."

The caller came back on the line. "Okay, it was rented to a Paul Fisher, in El Paso."

"Sir, give me his address and other information, but could you also fax me what you have so we can see the signature, and verify we're spelling it correctly?" Manny asked.

"Sure. His address and phone number are on the sheet, as well as his driver's license. My name, telephone number and address are at the top as well. There is one strange thing, however."

"What's that?" Manny asked.

"The destination given is Minnesota. That sure is a long way from Georgia," the man chuckled. "He must have had a big change in plans."

"Can you give me a description of the man who returned the van?"

"I wasn't here, but my attendant was. Hang on another minute, please. Hey, Ralph, do you remember what the man looked like? The guy who brought that white van and trailer in about three days ago...no? Okay. Sorry, Captain, he doesn't remember, but if he comes up with anything I'll let you know."

"When the man turned the vehicle in, did he rent something else, was anybody with him?"

"Ralph, come here will you. This is Captain Salinas on the line. He's asking questions that maybe you can answer."

"Hello. Hello, Ralph," Manny shouted into the phone shoving a fresh stick of gum between his lips.

"Yes, this is Ralph. You don't have to yell. What else do you want to know?"

"Anything. Anything about the man who turned in the van and trailer."

"Well, he said he was looking for another rental, a smaller vehicle, but we didn't have what he was looking for. I told him that maybe the agency down the road might have what he wanted. Does that help?"

Manny wanted to scream into the phone, that damn right it would help. "Listen, Ralph, that information would be very helpful.

What is the name of the agency you pointed him to, and just how far is down the road?"

"It's Harry's Bargain Rentals, and he's about a half-mile south of here."

— • • • —

Dani picked up the fax from the car rental dealer, went into her forensics' lab where it was quiet, and immediately dialed the number for Paul Fisher. After speaking with Mr. Fisher for several minutes it became clear this was a dead end.

Peaches lifted her head as Dani walked back into the team's open office space dubbed the bullpen. Manny followed the direction of Peaches' nose. "Whatcha got, Dani?" Manny stood up, hands on his hips.

"Well, good news and bad news. The good news is there is a Paul Fisher at this address. The bad news is he doesn't know anything about a van. He hasn't left the state of Texas in over twenty years. He can't imagine how his name got on a rental agreement, but then there had been some other weird things popup with his name. He was sent a speeding citation awhile back. Mind you, the ticket was dated when he was in the hospital recuperating from his heart attack. The driver's license the police officer wrote down was Mr. Fisher's."

"Isn't that interesting." Manny rubbed his neck as he mulled over what Dani said. "Maybe we're dealing with a stolen identity. George, call Harry's Bargain Rentals. See if a Mr. Fisher rented a car on the date the van was returned at the other agency, which just so happens to be the day after little Stephen was abducted. I'm going to call Cat and tell her I'm coming over, that we may have a lead."

"Captain, wait. Don't go yet," George called out. "I just got hold of Harry's Bargain Rentals. Dani, Dani come here. Manny, pick up line two again."

"Harry, Captain Salinas is on the line with us."

"Hello, Harry. Do you remember renting a car to a man on February 17?"

"Yes, I do. The reason I remember is because it was the only car I rented that day. Business has been real slow. If the economy continues going down, I just don't know if I can keep the agency open. ...yes, I have the paperwork right here."

"What did you rent to him?" Manny asked pacing back and forth at his desk. Peaches' head followed her master.

"A 2010 Ford Edge, silver gray. It has a Georgia plate. I'll fax this sheet to you. It was the best car on the lot. I don't know what I'm going to do."

"Yes, you said that. Your fax just came through. I see it has your name on it. I take it you're the owner of the company?"

"Yes, I am. And I'm proud to say I've been here for fifteen years. Now, I don't know if I'll be able to make it sixteen."

"I see you rented it to a Paul Fisher?"

"That's what it says. You'd think I'd remember him. I haven't had many customers lately, you know."

"How did he pay for the initial rental period?"

"MasterCard. It went right through."

"Well, Harry, thanks for the information. You've been very helpful. If we need any further information, I hope you don't mind if I call."

"Not at all. Anytime."

Chapter 20

— • • • —

CATHERINE AND LUCY sat at the kitchen table sipping their coffee. Neither spoke. They stared unseeing out the window, lost in their own thoughts. A cardinal perched on the bird feeder pecked at a couple of sunflower seeds and then flew away. Manny had called with news that there may have been a break in the case—he heard from a tipster. He asked Catherine to alert the reporters that she would have an update for them in two hours. Now, all she could do was wait for Manny to tell her what the tipster said.

The doorbell rang and Catherine quickly walked to answer it. The minute she opened the door Peaches muscled ahead of her master and sat in front of Catherine, waiting for her pat on the head as she vigorously dusted the floor with her tail.

"Yes, you're a pretty girl." Catherine gave her a pat and quick scratch behind her ears. Then she straightened up and looked Manny in the eye. "What did the tipster say?"

"Well, to paraphrase Dani, we have good news and some not so good news. But the good news is what's important."

"Come on in the kitchen, Manny, so Lucy can hear, too."

Lucy heard Catherine talking to the captain's dog, so she had a dog biscuit ready when they entered the kitchen. Peaches pranced right over to Lucy and carefully took the small treat from her fingers.

"Come on, Manny. Tell me what he said," Catherine said, pouring him a cup of coffee. Lucy refilled the cream pitcher and put out the sugar.

"A man called from Brunswick, Georgia, a car rental dealer. He heard on the news we were looking for a white van, possibly with a Texas plate. The day after Stephen was abducted, a man brought in a van fitting the description. The van had a trailer hitched to the back end. The dealer said he didn't call us right away because it never occurred to him that the white van on his lot could be the white van we were looking for. Then today he was sitting at his desk going through his paperwork, and the form the guy filled out when he returned the van came up. He said it hit him—white van, Texas plate—right there on the sheet of paper. He had the guy's name, a Paul Fisher, and address—lives in El Paso. Dani called the man, and this is the bad news. He hasn't been out of the state of Texas for years."

"But, then the tip doesn't mean anything," Catherine said, her shoulder's slumping.

"Ah, but wait a minute. The man wanted another rental but the dealer couldn't come up with what the guy was looking for so the dealer sent him down the road to another agency. He gave us the name and George called. The second dealer only rented one car that day, to none other than the same Paul Fisher. Cat, we think we've stumbled onto a couple of identity thieves."

"Oh, no. That could mean even more danger for Stephen." Catherine leaned back in her chair, closed her eyes, and immediately looked again at Manny. "So, do you have the description of the second car?"

"You bet I do. Here, I've written it out for you including the plate number. It's a 2010 Ford Edge SUV, silver gray, Georgia plate. When did you tell the reporters to be here?"

"Captain Manny, they're here now," Lucy said. "I just checked, and they're setting up their microphones."

"Manny, I have another picture of Stephen at his birthday party. It will pull on every mother's heartstrings—he's poking his finger in his cake. Also, I'm offering a hundred-thousand-dollar reward for information and conviction of this horrible person. How does that sound to you?"

"Excellent! The Amber Alert is already flashing the license tag number. When the reporters get hold of this information and the reward, it will be all over the airwaves within the hour, and every half-hour or so after that for at least today and tomorrow. And, this new information will keep the Amber Alert active for another five days. Cat, someone is bound to spot the car."

"I pray you're right, Manny. The longer I go without hearing he's been found...I don't know...the more frightened I am that something terrible has happened to him."

— • • • —

"Thank, God, we dumped that second car," Rafi said switching off the TV. "Pasha, cut up all the identification for Paul Fisher. Notice they didn't give a name, so they already know his cards were stolen. We can't use them anymore. You certainly were thinking when you put those extra Texas plates in the trailer before we left El Paso. Now that we have another car with any luck no one will track us down. They're looking for a silver gray Ford SUV you rented in Georgia, not our green Ford Escape I bought in Jacksonville. Where did you put the Florida license plate after you swapped it with the Texas plate on our new Escape?"

"It's in the attic with some of the others I brought with us," Pasha said.

"I rather like the irony that our new car is *an Escape*," Rafi said downing the last of his beer, a smile spreading across his face.

Chapter 21

— ••• —

AUGIE CRUISED DOWN to the ocean aboard his motorcycle. It was a perfect day for the last week of February. While the northern states were experiencing a cold snap, this day in Florida was beach weather. He had fifteen minutes to spare before rendezvousing with JJ. He wasn't sure where, within a thirty-six mile radius, JJ would be, but he was going to enjoy the tranquil lapping of the waves while plotting his next move.

Parking his Harley where the grass met the sand, but in plain sight so some wanna-be owner didn't get the bad idea of stealing it, Augie sat on the sand and thought about someday building sandcastles with Stephen. Pushing the thought from his head he punched in JJ's number.

"Yo."

"Yo, yourself. Did you get a picture of Sayid when he left last night?"

"Piece of cake. I released the men and they returned to their base in Miami. What did you find out?"

"Sayid reports to someone higher up. This man is coming in three days, ostensibly with the guy who is going to run the Detroit farm. But, he talked about setting up two more farms. They would be ready to go live after I train the farmers. In other words, they start production when I leave to go to the next city. It looks like we'll have the opportunity to bring down the entire ring in a coordinated raid."

"Whew. That will take some planning. How long do you figure we have before moving in?"

"Two weeks max. Maybe less. They seem to be on a tight timetable, because the identity documents have to be in the hands of the recruits, so the recruits can then infiltrate whatever the target is. I'm hoping I can learn more about the potential targets when I get to Detroit."

"Okay. Anything else?"

"You bet, potential problems. Did you catch the news an hour ago?"

"Yes. That Captain Salinas is pretty good. He found their vehicle and the car they replaced it with. Catherine is one strong woman—standing up there giving her plea again about not hurting her son. But, she's beginning to look drawn."

"Well, wouldn't you?" Augie snapped.

"Hey, it's me. I'm on your side. Remember?"

"What I'm worried about, is that they'll get a lead on our latest green car."

"Did you stick on the GPS, so we can follow it...if we have to?" JJ asked.

"Yes."

"Sorry, my man, I have to go now. I'm a worker-bee you know. I'm even getting a following for my killer Bloody Mary. I think it's the long, dill green bean instead of the celery."

— • • • —

Augie brushed the sand off his jeans, put on his helmet, and rode back to the house. Parking his bike, he heard Layla calling to him from the back door.

"Augie, are you going somewhere?" she asked.

"Just around the corner for some sandwiches."

"Hold on a minute. Stephen and I will come with you. I'll get your backpack." Layla reappeared in the doorway and walked down the front steps, handing Stephen to Augie.

"Come on little man, Augie is going to take you for a walk. Won't that be fun?" Augie took Stephen's pudgy hands and clapped them together. *Somehow I have to figure a way to return you to your mother,* he thought. "Now, into my backpack and up you go. No, Stephen, it's not time to play peek-a-boo. Come on. Take your hands off my eyes."

The baby giggled, playing the game a few more times before losing interest. He gave Augie a hug, wrapping his little arms around his neck and nestling his head against Augie's head.

"You really are good with him, Augie." *If only you were as attentive to me,* Layla thought.

"You know what, little man? It's past lunchtime and I'm starving. How about we go get a sandwich and an ice cream? How does that sound? Stephen, move your hands—I can't see. No ice cream then." Stephen giggled, pulled his hands back snuggling against Augie.

With Stephen bouncing up and down on his back and Layla trailing behind a few steps, Augie strode to the corner deli and ice cream parlor, made his purchases along with a few suggestions from Layla, and stepped out of the shop. Looking to his left to be sure he didn't bump into a tourist, he locked eyes with a man sitting on a bench in front of the bead shop. Augie abruptly turned to his right and headed for the corner. *Oh, my God. That was Pete.*

Walking as quickly as he could with Stephen's little arms tight around his neck, Augie rounded the corner and waited for Layla to catch up. "Here, take Stephen in the house and give him his sandwich. I'll be back in a minute. I forgot to pick up something."

Augie quickly swung Stephen down from his back putting him into Layla's outstretched arms. He crossed the street and continued walking with long strides. Fishing his cell out of his pocket, he punched in JJ's cell code at the same time taking a quick glance back down the street to be sure Layla had gone.

"Yep."

"JJ, I think I've been burned. Are you in the Palace Saloon?"

"Sure am."

"Hurry. There's a man sitting in front of the bead shop across the street. He's wearing a white blousy shirt and black pants. You have to ward him off. He could be calling the police right now as we speak. Bump into him and tell him to do nothing until you talk to him. JJ, be careful. Don't knock him over. He's a double amputee, fitted with prosthetics. His name is Pete Peterson— Daytona Pete. He helped us with our last mission, but you never met him. He carries a top-secret clearance. Tell him to meet you at the saloon. Hurry up!"

Augie returned to the house, opened the backdoor and entered the kitchen. Stephen was finishing his chocolate cone—more on his face and bib than probably went down his throat. Layla was putting the lunch items they'd just purchased out on the counter. Augie, wiping chocolate from Stephen's mouth, settled him in his highchair with some pieces of the tuna fish sandwich.

—•••—

"Oh, excuse me, sir. I'm sorry. I didn't mean to bump into you. Here, let me get that cell phone for you." JJ picked up the cell phone and looked straight into the man's face, their noses no more than three inches apart. "Your name Pete?"

The man whispered, "Yes." He didn't move a muscle or divert his eyes which bore holes into JJ's eyes.

"You may have thought you saw a friend of ours. He asked that you meet me, immediately, at the Palace Saloon across the street. Are you with someone?" JJ asked.

"Hey, Pete," Tillie called, coming out of the shop door. "Wait till you see—"

JJ left them, not looking back at the woman who had called to Pete. He calmly crossed the street and entered the saloon.

"Pete dear, who was that man?"

"A tourist, I think. He went to sit down and bumped into me. Nice enough chap. Now, sweet thing, what were you saying?" Pete asked. His mind was processing all that had happened within less than a minute. He could have sworn the man he saw, two stores down, was Hutch. And, the boy on his shoulders sure looked like Stephen, but he didn't have curls.

"I was saying that they have some beads from Africa that are spectacular. I told the shopkeeper I had to let my husband know I will be a little while longer. Pete, she said she'd give me all the information about her supplier, how to contact him, and best of all a back issue of his catalog."

"Well, you just do that. I think I'll go have a beer over at that saloon across the street. The Palace Saloon. I wonder if they have any dancing girls. Mercy, then I'd have to have two beers." Pete tried to chuckle, but he didn't sound convincing even to himself. "Don't hurry, little darlin'. I'll just be gabbing with the bartender."

"Okay, if you don't mind?"

"Run along and find out about those African beads. I know you've been looking for a supplier. It certainly would be cheaper than flying to Kenya."

— • • • —

Pete strolled over to the saloon. Pushing through the swinging doors he had to give his eyes a few seconds to adjust from the bright sunlight to the dim interior of the establishment. Two tables were occupied with couples, one having an animated conversation, and the other just seemed to want to rest. A woman sat at the bar, and Pete recognized the man who bumped into him behind the bar. Pete walked to the far end and sat on the last barstool, his eyes in a steely stare never left the bartender's face.

"What can I get you, sir," JJ asked returning Pete's penetrating stare.

"Information."

"One beer coming right up."

JJ pushed the spigot, expertly filling the glass with just the right amount of foam. "There you are, sir." JJ then leaned on the bar turning toward the kitchen in the back.

"It *was* him, wasn't it?" Pete hissed. "And, it was the kid! What the shit is going on?"

"It's a long story," JJ said quietly. "One we don't have time for at the moment. You have stepped into the middle of an operation. The child was grabbed without Hutch's knowledge. You have to believe that and trust that he will protect the boy."

"I thought he was dead."

"I know and so does everyone else. I was with him when he was shot. The medics lost him a couple of times before we reached the hospital. In a nutshell, he was unconscious for almost a week. When he woke up he was paralyzed from the neck down. Over the ensuing months he regained everything except his legs."

"Go on," Pete said, never averting his eyes from the bartender's face.

"The director, our boss, and I'm sure you know whom I'm referring to, said he was a valuable asset. All his old contacts and enemies thought he was dead. The director wanted him to come back to work, to insert him into a terrorist cell. Hutch agreed with one condition. He still wasn't sure if he would ever regain his health, and he made the director swear he would never tell Catherine that he was alive. He was consumed with guilt for almost getting her killed."

"And, how is his mother?" Pete asked.

"She's dead—did I pass your little test?" JJ replied.

"My wife could pop in here any minute. I have to know more. I want to hear this shit from him directly. I won't let on to anyone what I saw today, but I'll only keep quiet for twenty-four hours. I don't have to see him. I know the bastard's voice. Here's my cell number." Pete leaned over to get a small white paper napkin. "Mighty fine beer. Mighty fine, indeed," he said for the consumption of the few patrons. Pete wrote his number on the napkin and stood up to leave.

"Twenty-four hours. Otherwise I go to the police."

Chapter 22

— •••—

PETE SAT ON the balcony of his condo, looking out at the ocean. It was a bright starry night over Daytona Beach. The moon was in the west, but its beams played on the lapping waves and the beach below. He was sure if Hutch called him it would be after midnight. He zipped up his sweater to keep the night's cool air away from his body.

His thoughts skittered around in his head. Everything he knew for sure when he woke up this morning was now in question. Hutch probably didn't know he had married and Pete was pretty sure his friend had never met Tillie.

Tillie. The love of his life. Asleep in their bed. He was lucky to have found her. He loved her with every fiber of his being. He knew she loved him. She was so attentive, so aware of his needs when dealing with his handicap. He'd give her everything he owned, if it meant they would be together forever. "My darlin' Tillie," Pete mused. "Life would be so empty without you."

Pete hoped that somehow, his best friend, the man who stayed with him on the battlefield until the medics arrived, could somehow be reunited with Catherine and their son...their son. What a peculiar twist of fate that the little boy ended up in his father's arms.

Pete bowed his head, closed his eyes, and said a prayer. "Please, dear Lord, keep the little family safe, and somehow, someway, bring them back together."

The ring of his cell jerked Pete back to reality. He opened his phone. The name and number of the caller was *unknown*.

"Hey, big guy. You looked good today. Damn good," Hutch said.

"Well I might say the same for your sorry ass, but I can't bring myself to say anything nice to you."

"I understand. How's Catherine holding up?"

"All things considered, pretty well. No thanks to you."

"Pete, I can't tell you everything now, first of all there's no time, and second...I just can't. JJ said he filled you in a little. I must ask you, how close is Manny to finding Stephen?"

Pete inhaled quickly at Hutch's reference to the toddler. "A tipster in Georgia called in that he thought he might have the van the woman fled in from the airport with Stephen. Which brings me to the question...did you know you had a son?"

"No, not until I saw Catherine at the press conference. When she mentioned his birthday...I knew he was mine. I'd been told she married Manny."

"Shit. Back to the car. Manny believes an identity thief turned in the car. They traced the driver's license to a man in El Paso. Trouble is the man hadn't been out of the state for over twenty years. So, some guy turns in this van to a rental agency in Georgia. Was it you?"

"No. It wasn't me. Look, I can't talk long. The bartender you spoke with today, JJ. He was my operative in Venezuela in our last case, the one you helped us with. You can talk to him freely, but not to me. I can't take any chance on blowing my cover. This is big, Pete. Very big. I'm sick about the pain Catherine is in. I've racked my brains how I might get Stephen back to her. But there are extenuating circumstances, on my end, that make it impossible. At least, for now. On the other hand, he could be in even more danger if Manny stumbles on this mission. You must keep JJ posted if it looks as if Manny is getting close...if he finds out Stephen is on Amelia Island."

"I'll help if I can. This is one horrible situation, but I'd do anything to help Catherine get her son back...without any further harm done to him."

"If Manny gets too close, we may have to tell Catherine that I have Stephen and that I'm guarding him with my life...and...that I love her. Shit, Pete, what am I going to do?"

"Hey, buddy, hang on. This time it's my turn to save you...and your son."

Chapter 23

— • • • —

RAFI STOOD OUTSIDE the small, one-story terminal building to greet his visitor. The sleek Piper Jet aircraft landed softly on the Amelia Island airstrip. Masud swung his plane around and taxied to the fueling station. He wanted to be sure it was ready in the morning for his return flight to Detroit.

After fueling, Masud parked the plane in the designated area, climbed out with his carry-on bag, locked the plane's door, and ambled over to his friend. The two men hugged, and blew a kiss on each side of the other's face.

"You're looking well, Rafi," Masud said.

"I can say the same of you, Masud."

"How long has it been?"

"Almost six months since you bestowed on me the honor of testing your plan in Texas," Rafi answered. The men got into the car and Rafi drove to Fernandina Beach, leaving the asphalt runway behind. Ten minutes later, Rafi parked the car in front of the Florida House Inn and retrieved Masud's bag from the backseat. "I think you will like it here, Masud. Very peaceful, nobody pries into your business. I thought you could check in, and I'll wait for you in the courtyard out back for lunch. We can talk privately there. The afternoon sun will keep the air comfortable. As you requested, the whole team will join you for dinner."

"Quaint, very quaint. I can see why you like it here, Rafi. I'll do as you suggest and take my bag to my room. It shouldn't be more than a few minutes before I join you."

Rafi left Masud at the registration desk. He continued down the main hall and out into the courtyard where a few tables were set for luncheon service. Only one table was occupied by a couple with a child of about ten. Rafi indicated to the waiter he wanted the table off in the corner of the garden, the one on the right partially shielded with flowering bushes. He ordered two iced coffees with cream and sugar, and asked the young man to come back for his order when he saw his guest sit down. A gray cat brushed against his leg and then slowly walked into the surrounding vegetation, disappearing from sight.

Over lunch, the two friends talked about their families back in the Middle East and how different their lives were here in the U.S. Once the table was cleared and mugs of coffee set before them, Masud turned to Rafi. "Now, my friend, let's get down to business. Once a few of my acquaintances learned about our project, they contacted me with the type of people they were recruiting, and who would find identity documents useful. It seems there are many, shall we say, schemes percolating for the U.S. My friends require documents for a specific age range, men living in certain sections of the country, and of various ethnic backgrounds and skills. They require this so the recruits can operate freely say in Ohio, New York and surrounding states that are easily drivable in one day. I would say the majority should look Middle Eastern, but I have requests for Caucasians as well, almost any western country. There are also a few Asian computer scientists who will require documents. One thing my contacts stressed—no documents are needed for women. Let's say your farmers should harvest all beanstalks and no parsley." Masud chuckled.

"I presume the usual documents—Social Security cards, passports, credit cards, and especially driver's licenses—will be needed?" Rafi asked.

"Yes, but a resume of sorts, with some of the person's history would be helpful, if you can get it. Sayid told me of your work in this area. Very impressive."

"Pasha, Layla, and I have been doing some of the background research lately. Mainly to free up Augie's time, so he could process what we've harvested, but also so he could prepare for his trip to Detroit with you. We should be able to limp along until he returns. Augie is the best at getting backgrounds for the beanstalks," Rafi said grinning. "You will like him, Masud. He's rather unkempt, but a genius when it comes to researching the identity of the people we bring him from our harvest."

"I'm looking forward to meeting him. Sayid filled me in on how he has organized the research and the printing operation. In fact, your farm is working so well that I've asked Sayid to go ahead and build two more after Detroit is operational. So far, airports seem to give us an abundance of, what we call the beanstalks with the necessary DNA."

"Masud, using a print shop business as a front to our operation has worked well here. We have been accepted by the neighbors and we feel we can move around more freely than in El Paso."

"Then continue, my friend. I would think the shop also provides cover when, shall we say, our customers visit your business. Sayid and I have talked about this and are going to look for similar setups as we go forward with the farms."

"Where are you planning to locate the farms?" Rafi asked, taking a sip of coffee as he reached down to stroke the gray cat back again, now leaning against his leg.

"Detroit to start with, then obviously New York City, Tucson or Phoenix, and maybe Seattle and San Francisco."

"Lots of travelers entering and leaving those cities, that's for sure," Rafi said, sitting back in his chair. "And traveling to and from many countries."

"I want to send Augie to each city to set up the operations. He must travel to them, because, as you know, I won't allow our people to congregate in one place. If a farm is compromised, I don't want to risk everyone else going down with it."

"I couldn't agree more with what you say. How many are you planning to recruit?" Rafi asked.

"I believe around five-hundred to start."

"That many? Well, that will be quite a force for the American's to deal with...when you let them loose."

"Yes," Masud replied, a satisfied smile slowly spreading across his face. "Plans are being drawn up for their water system, the power grid, oil refineries, and nuclear plants, as well as various methods of mass transportation. The recruits will one-by-one infiltrate these organizations. These men on the inside will give us the plant layouts, where the vulnerabilities of the operations are, etcetera. Of course, they will also be ready to pull the trigger when the time comes. It will be a couple of years or more before we see the results of these initial harvests."

"Augie has taught me how to do the research and most of the printing, so he will be free to go wherever you need him on short notice," Rafi said.

"Good, because I plan to take him with me to Detroit when I leave tomorrow." Masud saw the surprised look on Rafi's face. "Do you have a problem with his leaving now?"

"No. I think not. Besides, I know he can advise us over the telephone if we run into any problems."

"Now, about your sister and the child. I think you should start to make plans for Layla to return home or to join her sister in Spain. I doubt the baby would be welcome in Pakistan, but she might raise him in Madrid. Is he dark skinned?"

"Not really, more an olive color. But he has very blue eyes."

"I still can't understand what possessed her to take the boy," Masud said, shaking his head. "I trust there is no suspicion or questions about her being the child's mother?"

"None. She thought it would help our cover here. You know, look like a real family. You'll see how well it works when they all join us for dinner. Speaking of which, I should get back to the shop. Because of the boy, we'll have to eat early, unless you would rather Layla not come with us?"

"No, no, I want to see how you all get along together."

"If you want to talk with Pasha and Augie after dinner, Layla can take the child home. It will be his bedtime." *I'm not going to mention that Layla is in love with Augie*, Rafi thought. *It would complicate everything.*

—•••—

"Shit." Augie put his headset down, stood up from his worktable, pushed his hair back from his eyes, and contemplated how he was ever going to be able to leave Stephen. The bug, under Rafi's favorite table at the inn, had relayed loud and clear Masud's plans. Augie texted JJ.

"i go 2 beach. we need 2 talk."
"when?" JJ replied.
"10 min."
"ok."

Augie jumped on his Harley, squealed away from the house heading to the beach. Within minutes he was sitting on the sand watching the waves roll in. His two-way radio signaled JJ was ready to hear why Augie was upset. Of course, he too had listened to the conversation between Masud and Rafi and was expecting Augie's call—the call came through two minutes before JJ expected.

"You heard?" Augie snapped, still staring at the waves.

"Yes man. How do you want to play it?"

"What am I going to do? Leave Stephen unprotected? My God, how can I?"

"It's rough."

Augie stood up brushing the sand off the seat of his pants. He straightened up. "Well, goddamn it, here's the plan. You talk to the director. Tell him two things have to happen or he can extract me from the farm right now."

JJ sighed in relief. Here was the tough agent he knew. "Give 'em to me."

"You tell him that as of this moment, Matt Baker is assigned to Stephen."

"Baker's a good man. He looks like a grandfather. No one would guess he is an undercover agent," JJ replied.

"Well, just remember, you are Stephen's guardian angel and Baker is his guardian. If Layla takes him to the store, the park, or even the backyard, Baker is to have his eyes on him. Until Baker arrives on Amelia Island you stay with Stephen. Let me know when Baker reports to you. Until then, you and I will communicate by cell. Once he's on board and your replacement arrives you'll be able to join me. Sounds like that will be somewhere in Detroit."

"What's number two on your list?"

"It looks like three to four weeks more of this shit before we can pull the raid. So I think you'd better give Pete the go ahead to tell Catherine what's happening. I trust her to keep the information to herself. Hell, both Stephen's and my life will depend on it. There are three people in this world I trust implicitly—you, Pete, and Catherine."

"Done. So there won't be any second guessing, I'll put my job on the line and give Pete the go ahead to talk to Catherine before I ask the director's permission. How do you like that?"

"JJ, you're the best. I love you, man."

"Whoa, let's not get carried away, smart ass."

"Listen up, Mr. Bartender. Keep your big ears open at five-thirty. We're all going to have dinner at the inn. We may learn more of Masud's bigger plans that are designed to strike at the very core of our country."

Chapter 24

— ••• —

CATHERINE WONDERED WHY Pete asked to meet with her privately, at her house. Hearing the doorbell, she walked to the front door to greet him. *I guess I'll find out soon enough,* she thought. Stepping inside, Pete gave Catherine a peck on her cheek.

"Thanks for seeing me, Catherine, on such short notice."

"You said you wanted to talk to me alone, so let's go in the library. I asked Lucy to bring us some coffee unless you'd like something else?"

The morning sun pierced the large French doors and windows along one side of the library, beckoning the eye out to the garden. Opposite the windows was a wall of cherry bookcases—a small television, books, pictures of Stephen filled the shelves. The cases were topped with mementos and treasures from Catherine's travels.

"No. Coffee is fine. How're you holding up?" Pete asked.

"Some hours are better than others, but I still have a sense of helplessness. Please, sit wherever you feel most comfortable. The Amber Alert expires tomorrow and even the media has all but given up. They tell me as soon as I have a new lead they'll run the story again with Stephen's picture."

Pete chose a straight chair facing Catherine across her cherry butler's table. He avoided big, soft, cushy couches or chairs. They were hard for him to leverage his feet to stand up when wearing his prosthetics.

Lucy brought in a tray with a carafe of coffee, mugs, and cream and sugar. She set it on the coffee table. "Hello, Mr. Pete. Anything else I can do for you, Miss Catherine?"

"No, this will be fine. Thanks, Lucy."

"How are you, Lucy?" Pete asked.

"To tell you the truth, Mr. Pete, not so good. The house is quiet, too quiet. I...I...excuse me." Lucy hurried out the door, unable to hold back the onslaught of tears.

Pete looked over at Catherine with pain in her eyes as she watched Stephen's nanny leave the room.

"I'm sorry, Pete. On the whole, Lucy and I try to bolster each other up, but sometimes the fear is overwhelming. Now, what is it that you want to talk privately about? I hope nothing's wrong with Tillie?"

"Oh, no, my darlin' is wonderful as ever. Catherine, the day you introduced me to Tillie was the best day of my life. I thank you forever for that."

"I'm happy for both of you. So, is there some emergency with one of the franchises?"

"No, no. The division is doing well." Pete stood, moving to the couch. He sat on the edge at the other end facing Catherine. "Catherine, totally by accident, I find myself in the middle of something. I have to share with you...ah, some information. But, the hard part is that you and I can be the only ones who know what I'm about to tell you. Catherine, lives depend on putting our trust in others. You are the type of woman who wants to take hold of a situation, to solve a problem, 'come hell or high water,' as my dad used to say."

"Pete, I really am not following you. What is it that only you and I can know? You sound like Hutch, when he tried to explain that there would be times he couldn't tell me where he was, or what he was doing. That there may be days or weeks he wouldn't be able to communicate with me for fear of jeopardizing his mission, or worse, his men might be killed." Catherine's emotions bubbled up talking about her lover. She dug in her jean's pocket for a tissue. "I'm sorry. It's just—" She took a deep breath and looked back at Pete. "All he could really tell me was that he was an agent for the government—not what department, not which branch, and certainly nothing about his mission."

"That's exactly what I'm trying to say. I'm asking you to trust me, literally with your life, and others, if I tell you what I stumbled into. Can you do that, Catherine? Can you trust me that much without knowing what I'm going to say? Knowing that it will be one of the hardest trusts you will ever be asked to grant. Your knowing, but refraining to act, will be excruciating. Can you trust me, Catherine?" Pete picked up her hand and held it tightly with both of his. He looked into her eyes, eyes that stared back at him, trying to comprehend what he was asking of her.

"Is this to do with Stephen?" she asked clenching Pete's hand.

"Yes!"

"Then, please, go on. I promise you I will follow your lead. Hutch once told me that you were his best friend...that he would trust you with his life, so I can do no less."

Pete put her hand back in her lap. He looked straight into her piercing brown eyes. "Stephen is alive and well. I saw him."

"My baby's okay?" she whispered not daring to move, the words strangling in her throat. She continued to look straight at Pete, her eyes questioning. "Where is he? When can I get him?"

Pete managed to stand, walked a couple of steps, swung his arms, punching his fist into his hand. "The woman who abducted him is a member of an identity theft ring."

Catherine returned Pete's gaze with a puzzled look on her face. "Why would she want to get entangled with kidnapping?"

"She evidently thought it would help the group's cover...if they looked like a family. There are several members in this ring."

"Well, why can't the authorities, who I presume are trying to break up this ring, just arrest them, and bring Stephen home? I don't understand, Pete. Why would that be out of the question?" she asked her voice rising. "Well?"

"The ring is involved in homeland security issues, big issues. The agents must identify all the players before moving in. They can't be premature or they won't be able to stop them."

"Oh, my God, and Stephen is in the middle of this ring?" Catherine put her head in her hands, covering her eyes, and then abruptly looked up. "Why are you telling me this? So far I don't see any connection with what you've told me except that I'm the mother of the little boy who was kidnapped."

"Manny has tracked down the van they used. The group turned in the van because it was hot, and now they have another vehicle, which you know about, and told the public about at your last press conference. If Manny stumbles on the ring, they will flee. Go underground. The agents may have trouble finding them again. Finding Stephen."

"Pete, where did you see Stephen? Where did you see my son? And what makes you think they won't harm him, or worse, kill him?" Catherine was now standing, following Pete around the room.

Pete turned to face Catherine. "Homeland Security inserted Hutch into the ring!"

Catherine's jaw dropped, her eyes opened wide in disbelief, she couldn't breathe. "I don't believe you," she stammered. Catherine paced to the window, turned back and faced Pete. "Whatever makes you think you can come into my home and tell me such a pack of lies. How stupid do you think I am?" She yelled at Pete. She yelled at herself. What was Pete saying? Is Hutch alive? No. He's dead!

Pete walked to her, wrapped his arms around her, and held her tight against her struggles. "Yes, Catherine, Hutch is alive. The doctors somehow brought him back from the dead that fateful night. They saved him. He was unconscious for days, and when he woke up he was paralyzed. He made his friend, JJ and his boss, swear they would never tell you or his mother that he was alive. He was full of guilt because you were almost killed. He couldn't move from his shoulders down. He wanted to die." The words tumbled out of Pete's mouth, he couldn't hold them back another second.

Catherine went limp in Pete's arms, sobbing uncontrollably. He eased her back to the couch, sat next to her, never letting go. "Catherine, he loves you. He wants to return to you. He saw your first news conference, when you talked about Stephen's birthday. Hutch figured out that Stephen is his son."

Chapter 25

— • • • —

DINNER WAS LIVELY—laughter, stories of their experiences dealing with the American culture, and Stephen pulling on Masud's beard, squealing with delight. The air was still and cool, but heavy sweaters kept them comfortable. Tiny white lights adorned many of the bushes turning the inn's courtyard into a romantic fantasy world. The inn's two gray cats romped gaily between the tables, circling around and between the legs of some of the guests. Everyone let down their guard just a little, helped along with a few extra drinks. Layla finally excused herself, and took the still giggling child home to his bed.

"Oh my, I haven't laughed, or enjoyed myself this much for a long time," Masud said, wiping tears of laughter from his eyes with his handkerchief. In a quiet voice, he added, "I can understand what Layla meant about presenting a family. I noticed some of the guests looked our way smiling because of the lad."

After Masud told Augie to be ready for an early morning departure, the men each had a cup of coffee, laced with Amaretto, and then said goodnight. Rafi stayed behind to have a few last words with Masud and to make arrangements to drive him to the airstrip in the morning. Both Pasha and Augie went home to their bedrooms.

— • • • —

The house was quiet. Augie stripped down to his shorts and slipped under the sheets. He heard Layla entering his room before he saw her. She climbed into bed with him, curling around his back, her free hand stroking his arm.

"Augie. Augie, are you awake?" she whispered in his ear with a kiss.

"Yes, I'm awake, but I'm tired, Layla. Go back to your room so we can both get some sleep."

"Augie, it was nice tonight, yes? Masud got a kick out of Stephen don't you think?" Layla continued to stroke his arm, then fished her hand under his arm playing with the hair on his chest. "Augie, I know you like me. We make a nice family—you, me, and little Stephen. Yes?" she said softly, her warm breath on his back.

Augie turned to face her, leaning on his elbow. He realized too late that he had made a tactical mistake. Layla moved against his body, kissing him passionately, rolling over on top of him.

"Augie, I love you," she said between kisses. "Augie, I want you to make love to me. I want you, Augie. I know you want me. Look at me, Augie," she said pulling her silky white nightgown off over her head, her shiny, long black hair cascading around her shoulders, and touching Augie's chest. "I'm beautiful, yes? Augie, look at me. Love me." She pressed her body to his, kissing him deeply, her breasts pressed against him as her hand traced down his body.

"Layla, stop this." He rolled her onto her back as gently as he could, pinning her arms to her side. "Layla, you are a very attractive woman. Yes, I like you, but I'm not ready for this...for a relationship with you. Masud wants me to leave with him early in the morning to set up a farm like ours. Now is not the time for you—"

"You, bastard. You just don't want me. You might as well spit on me. I bring you a child. I thought we could be a family. Well, you're not good enough for Stephen and me. No more Layla for you," she hissed, fishing around the bed for her nightgown. She crawled quickly from his bed, stomped to the door. She turned to look back at him, full of fury. "Take a look at what you turned away. This was your last chance to be a family. You'll see. There won't be another one." She flung the silky gown at him and left his room, slamming the door behind her.

Augie grabbed his cell off the nightstand the noise of the slamming door ringing in his ears. He scrunched down under the sheet, his breath ragged, waiting to see if Pasha or Rafi came to investigate the disturbance. The house remained quiet. He punched in JJ's code.

"Hey, this is cozy. Nothing like a call from my partner when I'm in the middle of a dream with a beautiful redhead."

"Shut up and listen. I just had a bad scene with Layla. She might do something foolish. I'm leaving in the morning with Masud. Tell Baker I'm depending on him to see no harm comes to my son. And, JJ..."

"Yes boss."

"Remember, you're Stephen's guardian angel."

Chapter 26

—•••—

AS THE SUN breached the horizon the next morning, Augie pushed open the door to the bedroom now occupied by Stephen. He tiptoed to the side of his crib. Stephen had his bear clutched tightly to him, his little mouth slightly open as he breathed rhythmically. *You are such a little angel,* Augie thought. *Daddy has to go away for a few days, but I'll be back.* "I love you, Stephen." Augie bent over placing his lips on his son's soft downy cheek. The child moved a little in response to the touch of his father's lips, but he did not wake up.

Augie left the room, closing the door quietly behind him, leaning back against it for a moment eyes closed, and then headed to the kitchen. He put on a pot of coffee and waited for Rafi to join him before they left to pick up Masud at the inn for the short drive to the plane.

—•••—

Augie was packed and ready to accompany Masud to Detroit. Traveling with Masud, he hoped to glean a bigger picture of the operation and his plans for terrorist acts. He also wanted to get away from Layla for awhile. Maybe her romantic inclinations toward him would dissipate. The worst part of leaving Amelia Island was that he would have to trust Layla with the care of his son.

Masud was all business at the controls of the aircraft heading to a small airport in the Detroit area. Augie sat in the co-pilot seat, but he gave no indication that he knew how to fly a plane. Where the night before at dinner Masud seemed to be chatty, today he was tight lipped. Once in awhile he pointed out a place of interest on the land below, but that was it. Augie decided it would not be good to appear too inquisitive, so he remained quiet as well. He excused himself to take a trip to the lavatory. Returning to the cockpit, he pressed a bug to the bottom of the co-pilot seat and then settled back. He appeared to be sleeping, but his mind was spinning.

Approaching Michigan, Masud opened up a little, confiding to Augie about the buildup he anticipated in the Detroit document operation. "When we land, Aboud will meet us at the plane. He is the farm leader, same as Rafi. The difference is that Aboud is extremely good on the computer. He has no problem downloading the day's harvest and doing the research, matching full documentation with a name. He seems to find the backgrounds of those harvested quickly."

"How about the preparation of the documents, and the equipment and supplies needed for printing?" Augie asked.

"That's why we need you to make the farm fully operational. The harvest, of course, catches people traveling back and forth from Canada, as well as other destinations. But those returning to Canada are also very interesting, as we will be able to initiate a farm on the other side of the border with fully documented, shall we say, Canadians."

"It shouldn't take more than two days, three tops, to bring him up to speed, especially if he's as savvy as you seem to think. I already have a dealer waiting with the electronic devices, and the various papers, passport covers, and inks. I'll take Aboud to meet him when we pick up the initial equipment and supplies. How many men does Aboud have to help in the operation?" Augie asked.

"Three. Same as Amelia Island."

"Okay. While the research for the backup information is what takes the time, the preparation of the documents and the printing can be tricky. Do you think his recruits are up to the production process?" He hoped he wasn't pushing too hard but it seemed like a necessary question.

"Aboud is hopeful, with your training, two of his men will be able to handle the production. Aboud could do it all but that would slow the whole operation down. We will ask you for your opinion of their skills after you have spent a couple of hours with them— your opinion as to whether or not they can handle the assignment."

"Of course."

"If not...well, they'll have to go home. With the missions ahead, we have to include only smart, capable men who can think on their feet. You know, improvise when an operation doesn't proceed exactly as planned."

The conversation ended as Masud talked to a man on the ground for permission to land. He brought the jet down, and taxied to some structures used as makeshift hangars able to shelter a few planes in inclement weather, particularly the winter snowstorms.

A man stepped forward to the parked aircraft, giving a warm greeting to Masud, who introduced the man to Augie. The large, bearded man was Aboud. As before, no one used or asked for a last name.

Chapter 27

—•••—

IT WAS A SLOW afternoon at the Palace Saloon. JJ's replacement had checked in and was off to rent a room, leaving JJ to tend bar for the last time before joining Augie. A silver-haired man, bright gray eyes, sauntered through the swinging saloon doors. He was dressed in a long-sleeved, black turtleneck shirt over tan cargo pants.

"Hey, bartender, I hear you make a mean Bloody Mary," the gentleman called out.

"You heard right, mister. Have a seat while I stir up the meanest Mary you ever had."

The man went to the far end of the bar putting his feet up on the rail of the barstool next to him. "I don't want any of that bushy shit. I want one of those garlicky-dill green beans. In fact, make that a couple. Oh and bartender add extra salt around the rim of that glass."

"You got it." JJ fixed the man's drink, put a paper coaster in front of him and set the tall glass down. "Now, take a sip of that and tell me if it isn't the meanest Mary you ever put your lips on."

"Umm. I think you may be right." The man leaned in over the bar and whispered, "Good to see you again, JJ. I ran into your replacement. He said you're leaving tonight."

JJ leaned on the bar, faced the kitchen. "Nice to see you, too, Matt. Welcome to Amelia Island and the Palace Saloon."

"The director said you'd fill me in on my assignment. For some reason he chuckled when he said it. So give it to me."

"Well, you are to watch the back of someone caught in the middle of a sting. Watch and make sure nothing happens to him. He's blonde, blue eyes, and—"

"What's his name?"

"Stephen. Stephen Hainsworth, and—"

"How old is he? Tall, skinny, what?"

"Well, he's one."

"One what...thirty-one, fifty-one?"

"No, just one and well, maybe a couple of months. Not very tall—"

Matt Baker cocked his head, his lips drawn up in a smirk, eyebrows raised. "Okay, you've had your fun now give it to me straight."

JJ reached in his pocket and pulled out a picture of Augie with Stephen on his back.

"That's Hutch. I thought he was dead."

"Yes, well, let's keep it that way. It took him over a year and a half to recover from his wounds. The director felt he was perfect for this assignment, so he was dropped into a terrorist plot—"

"That part the director did layout, just not my part in this little play. I thought you were Hutch's contact."

"I am. Your assignment is to guard the other person in the picture."

Matt looked at the picture again. He stared back at JJ, brow furrowed, eyes questioning.

"The little boy is Hutch's son. He lives with the gang who make up the cell, here on the island. A woman, Layla, is posing as his mother and we fear, no, make that we know she's unstable. Plus when we pull the raids, we, *you*, have to be sure to extricate the baby unharmed. I'll meet you on the beach in an hour and fill you in. Then I'm off to Detroit to hookup with Hutch again. It's imperative you and I communicate several times a day...let me know what's happening."

"Okay, but why not just when there seems to be a change?"

"Because, shithead, Hutch keeps asking me if the kid is all right. We can't have his mind wandering around...he has to focus...these are bad people he's working with."

Matt looked down at the picture again and then stuffed it in his pant pocket. "He sure is a cute little guy. I didn't know that Hutch was married."

"He's not. Not yet, anyway. Being shot kinda messed up his personal life, if you catch my drift. There's a bar across the street from the house where they, the gang, are holed up. I thought maybe you could play the part of an eccentric author, you know, hang out at the bar, click away on your laptop, but keeping your eyes on the house."

"Sure, that could work, except for the eccentric part. Although, I always thought I might look good with a beard, maybe grow a ponytail..."

Chapter 28

—•••—

THE NEXT TWO DAYS sped by quickly. Masud was right. Aboud was a very quick study. One of his recruits picked up on the production process as if he'd been printing all his life. Augie had a chance on the second day to plant a bug under the desk that carried the telephone. He never put a bug in the telephone. It was a custom, dictated by Sayid, to check the phones periodically for just such a device. This check really was a waste of time, as they rarely used anything but their cell phones.

Back on Amelia Island, the new agent had replaced JJ who was already in Detroit. Augie had texted him with the location of the Detroit farm. So far, mimicking the success of the setup on the Island, Aboud had rented a house with a store front. They lived and operated their business inside the same structure.

Early in the morning of the second day, Augie left the farm for his routine jog. He passed run-down houses intermixed with run-down stores—a grocer, consignment shop, and liquor store with bars on the windows and entrance. His mind wandered back to the idyllic time he had spent with his son on Amelia Island, eating ice cream, and window shopping in the village of Fernandina Beach. He longed to be there again, but this time with Catherine as well. Shaking his head in an attempt to clear his thoughts, he pulled his cell out of his lower right cargo pants pocket and hit JJ's code.

"Yo, partner."

"Did you find a room in the neighborhood?" Augie asked.

"Yes, but I hope we won't be here long. Me and the roaches are not exactly the best of friends. I'm just eight houses north of you, gray siding, same side of the street. Come to think of it, they all look gray."

"Any word from Baker? Stephen okay?"

"Yes. Baker's got Stephen's back, his little back," JJ said trying unsuccessfully to make light of a difficult situation for his friend.

Ignoring JJ's remark, Augie asked, "Any word from Pete?"

"Nothing."

Chapter 29

— • • • —

MOONBEAMS LIT THE sky as Layla swiftly drove over the causeway leaving Amelia Island behind her. Little Stephen slept in his car seat. He didn't even wake up when Layla had carefully lifted him from his crib and put him in the car, tucking in a blanket to protect him from the night's cold air. She had planned her escape over the last several days, ever since Augie had refused her advances. It had been humiliating. *Well, he would never get the chance again to make love to me,* she thought. Hell, none of the men at the farm respected her, and the leader, Sayid, looked down on her with disdain. Masud thought the child was cute, but it was only a matter of time until he turned on her.

"Well, who needs them," she whispered to Stephen. Tears streamed down her face and she continually slapped the steering wheel as the car barreled west on Interstate 10. Pulling another tissue from the box, she thought, *those bastards think they're so smart. Well I have lots of credit cards and I know how to use them. Rafi told me many times that the recruits were trained to draw the maximum amount of cash at one time from the ATM machines, buy whatever you need all in one day, then cut them up and throw them in the trash.*

If the law was on the lookout, watching for someone to use a particular card, she would be long gone. Augie was clever in figuring out their person pins enabling access into the accounts. Usually, he found it was a birthday, or a child's name. If he couldn't find it that way, he had a dictionary program that pulled it up if the pin was a word. Other times he hacked into a computer and found it. What did she care how he did it as long as she had the pin.

Oh, yes, she thought, *I learned all their little tricks.* When she decided to leave the farm, she took two of the license plates Pasha had stored in the attic. They were still current so an officer would have no reason to pull her over. Once she decided where she was going to stay, maybe even rent a little house, she would put the Florida plate back on and sell the car, or ditch it. *No,* she thought, *I'd rather sell it so I'll have the money.* After disposing of the car one way or another, she would rent a car.

Layla had driven for several hours when the sun rose behind her. Stephen started to cry. He was hungry and so was she. Seeing a billboard for a Denny's at the next exit, she followed the signs and pulled in. It felt good to stop driving. Grabbing her map of the southern states, and lifting an unhappy baby from his car seat, she went into the restaurant.

The waitress was very helpful and immediately brought a highchair to the table. Layla pulled a Sippy cup from Stephen's bag and the waitress filled it half full with milk and gave him some soda crackers. Layla knew her eyes were swollen from crying, so she kept her dark glasses on. Her earlier hunger pangs now subsiding, she didn't feel much like eating so she ordered some snacks for the road—a couple of sandwiches, cartons of juice for Stephen, and some cracker packets. With Stephen happily eating bits of banana, Layla checked her map. She'd made good time and it looked like she could make Mobile, Alabama, in less than three hours. That certainly would be enough driving for one day.

Without checking her wallet, she knew she had plenty of cash for their meals and a motel, enough for a couple of days anyway. Once she settled in for the night, she would plan her next move. She'd make a list tonight of what she had to have for the next few days. She didn't need much for herself. Her jeans and T-shirts would do while she was driving. The heavy sweater she grabbed at the last minute would do for now...an outfit or two for Stephen were a must, along with some disposable diapers, and more snacks for traveling.

Tomorrow, once she was in Mobile, she'd hit an ATM machine and go on a buying spree. Fortunately, the farm had let her keep Stephen's stroller in the car...after all she did all the grocery shopping so she needed it with her.

"They'll be sorry I'm gone, Stephen. No one to buy the food, let alone cook their meals, or do their laundry. They never appreciated what I did for them." And Augie. Well, Augie was missing a good thing. She knew she had a beautiful body, for all the good it had done her. Layla could feel a fresh batch of tears coming so she quickly paid the check, put Stephen back in his car seat, and continued west.

Chapter 30

—•••—

AUGIE HAD NOT been in touch with the director since leaving the hospital in New York for his new assignment. He knew JJ was relaying information, but it wasn't the same as hearing it from the man playing the part. JJ told him the director was getting antsy—he wanted the personal touch. Aboud had been his shadow every minute since arriving in Detroit. He had to figure out an excuse to leave the house before Masud flew him to the New York farm. Augie packed his duffel bag which took all of ten minutes. Not much to pack—he always traveled light.

Joining the group in the kitchen, Augie poured himself a cup of coffee. He leaned against the counter and addressed Aboud. "Do you have any questions for me before I leave?"

"No. I think you covered everything. But when I checked our supplies last night I found we're running low on ink and the special card stock."

"Would you like me to run over to the dealer?" Augie asked. "I have time. Masud said he needed to make a few phone calls before we leave."

"Could you? That would help a lot. I'm in the middle of a search and want to keep digging." Aboud didn't look up, his fingers flying over the keyboard.

"No problem. I'll leave now and be back in less than an hour," Augie said.

—•••—

Borrowing Aboud's car, Augie drove to a nearby strip mall which was located near the dealer who carried the farm's production supplies. He pulled into a parking space at the end, retrieved his cell and punched in the private number the director had given him.

"Well, my friend, it's been a long time since we talked," the director said.

"Yes sir, well, it took a little more time than I thought to get Pat and Mike to cooperate. I'm sure JJ's been filling you in."

"Indeed he has. Of course, I would like to hear from your lips about this farming operation."

"I don't have much time, so I won't repeat what I'm sure JJ has told you. Yes, they call the location of their production of the personal identification documents a farm. I'm a mile from the Detroit farm now. I was assigned to train and organize their procedures. By the way, the men working the Detroit farm are very skillful, both technically with the computer and the printing process. JJ has their pictures and names."

"Clever that they don't use anybody's last name," the director said.

"It's my guess that only Masud and Sayid have the full dossiers of each person, and I'm not sure about Sayid. Masud is flying me to an airstrip outside of New York City, where another farm has just been staffed with fresh recruits."

"Are you to train these men as well?"

"Yes, and check the equipment and supplies. Then we leave for Tucson which, I'm told, will be the last stop. I hope we can round up the bastards. The sooner the better. Don't forget, they killed a man named Johnny for breaking some crazy farm rule in El Paso."

"You must be careful, son."

"One more thing. I could be paranoid, but there are times when I catch Masud staring at me. It's like he's trying to figure me out, or maybe he thinks he saw me somewhere. I don't know. But if I give a call for help, I want it immediately. Do we understand each other?"

"Yes, of course. JJ has your back, plus each house is under surveillance when you give us the location. The bugs you are planting are also a big help but they tend to use their cell phones, so if they talk outside we don't hear what is being said."

"Okay. I gotta go. Two more farms to set up and then I hope you bring me in. Bring me in with my little boy."

—•••—

"Aboud, you're a natural. I came to show you how to find information and ended up with your teaching me a few tricks. Good job. As you said this morning, I think I've done all I can here. The production operation seems to be going well, so I don't think you'll have any problems. If you do, just give me a call," Augie said, smiling.

"It was a pleasure to learn from someone so accomplished and organized," Aboud said, shaking Augie's extended hand. "Masud and I talked this morning, and I think he's going to escort you to the New York farm, probably early tomorrow morning."

"That sounds great—I'm ready to go. If you'll excuse me, I'll call Rafi on the island to see how things are going. Are we all eating dinner together tonight?" Augie asked.

"Yes, and it is about time for dinner," Masud said, entering the workshop.

"Aboud indicated that you're ready to fly me to the New York farm," Augie said.

"That's right. Tomorrow. I want to leave a couple of hours before dawn. Flying into that morning sunrise is a killer. You go ahead and call Rafi, and then we'll walk down to our favorite Italian restaurant."

Augie caught the beginning of their conversation as he left to make his call. "Aboud, I have a recruit coming tomorrow with the plans for the reservoir system, and—"

—•••—

Augie went to the kitchen, poured himself a cup of coffee, and sat down at the kitchen table. He pulled out his cell and called Rafi.

"She what? Layla left?" Augie yelled into the phone. He was now on his feet, pacing the room, rubbing his head, pulling his hair back from his eyes. "Rafi, slow down. I can't understand what you're saying."

"Layla took the car sometime last night. She took the kid with her. She hasn't been the same since you left, Augie. She left a note on the kitchen counter."

"Goddamn it. What does the note say?" Augie snapped, trying to lower his voice so he didn't alarm Masud.

"Let me read it to you," Rafi said.

> "My dear Rafi,
>
> I can't take this life anymore. I know Sayid is very unhappy with me for complicating the mission with little Stephen. I had hoped that Augie might see we could be a family. Rafi, I love Augie more than life itself, but he doesn't acknowledge I exist. I cannot be around him any longer, and I know you men don't want me anyway.
>
> Rafi, I'm leaving and taking the baby with me. He is nothing but a burden to everyone on the farm. I don't know where I'm going. Once I'm settled, I'll let you know where I am. But I will do this only if you promise not to bring me back to the farm or send me home.
>
> I have my documentation papers and many credit cards so I should be fine until I settle and find a job. Please wish me well as I wish you.
>
> Your loving sister, Layla"

"That's it, Augie," Rafi said. "It's now been almost two days and I have no idea which direction she went. Maybe it's for the best. I'll wait until she gets back in touch with me. I've already told Sayid, and he says he's relieved."

With all the control he could muster, Augie said, "I suppose you're right, Rafi. Let me know if you hear from her."

—•••—

"Damn it, JJ, Layla's left the farm and she took Stephen with her. Tell me you know where she is."

"I just had a call from Matt and—"

"Does he know where she is? Is he following her? Is Stephen okay? Come on, man, give me some answers."

JJ took a deep breath. "Yes, Matt's following her. He did have a few anxious hours because she left in the middle of the night. When he finally noticed the car was gone, gone longer than it would take to run to the grocery store, he called the Staties. It took them an hour, in coordination with the Alabama officers, to find the car. He knew she either took Interstate 95 north or south, or I-10, running west. Seems she's heading west. Matt took off, turned onto I-10 west, and gunned the heck out of his car. He finally got in range of the GPS you put under her rear bumper and locked on."

"He must have been hours behind her. Where did he catch up with her?" Augie asked his stomach lurching, turning into knots.

"In Mobile. He tracked her to a motel and got a room. He also stuck a motion device under her car so if she pulled a middle-of-the-night escape again, he'll get a signal that the car is moving."

"Shit, JJ, I was afraid she was going to take off. She left a note for Rafi saying she felt nobody appreciated her, especially yours truly. She doesn't know where she's going, but she said she'd be in touch with him once she knows."

"Do you want me to call Pete? And, what about Catherine?"

"If I have any chance to be part of Catherine's life again, she has to be told what's happening. She would never forgive me if she thought I was holding out on her."

"Okay, I'll call Pete. But first, partner, I have to call the director and let him know about these extenuating circumstances."

"I talked with him today. When you call him, please tell him I was not aware of Layla's fleeing, really kidnapping Stephen for the second time. Let me know once you talk to him and to Pete, and especially Matt. Masud wants to leave early in the morning so you'll have to text me."

— • • • —

"Matt, you there? Speak up," JJ yelled into the phone.

"Ya man, I'm here. Why are you yelling at me?"

JJ sighed. "Everyone's been yelling at me so I thought I'd yell back," he said calmly. "You know, that felt pretty good."

"I'm happy for you," Matt said. "Now let me fill you in on my situation so I can get some sleep before the beautiful Layla decides to leave again."

"Good. Fire away."

"As you know, I had to pull some strings with local law enforcement, local as in the states of Florida and Alabama. She's now tucked in a motel for the night."

"Are you sure she has the baby with her?"

"I haven't seen him, but from the looks of the mess in the car—kids sure do love those crackers—I'd stake my life on it."

"Yes, well text me in the morning once you've eye-balled him or your life as you know it may be over."

Chapter 31

—•••—

SNOWFLAKES, HEAVY WITH moisture, were falling. Augie checked his clock—1:35 a.m. Still several hours before Masud would head to his plane. Looking out his bedroom window onto the garbage pickup road in back of the house, he thought he caught three shadows in the neighbor's back porch light. He continued watching to see if the shadows returned. At the sound of a light tap on his door, Augie turned as Aboud stuck his head in, finger to his lips signaling to be quiet.

Suddenly they heard a loud crash from their print shop. Aboud ran to the stairs. The other two farmers stormed out of their room and followed Aboud down the stairs, guns drawn. Augie followed suit, but several steps behind. Masud stepped out of his room and walked behind Augie, his hand on Augie's back as they crept down the staircase. At the bottom of the stairs, they could hear men in the shop swearing up a storm in loud whispers, pulling out drawers and emptying the contents on the floor with the aid of several flashlights.

Aboud switched on the fluorescent shop lights, his gun pointed at two men, heads covered with black ski masks. "Get out of here, you sons-a-bitches," he yelled. The two farmers charged the would-be robbers, smashing their fists into noses and chests as the robbers struggled to get to the door, all the time screaming in pain, and yelling not to hurt them. The shop door burst open, their screaming and hollering continued as they tried to get their footing in the slushy snow.

In the distance sirens could be heard, then flashing red lights. "Shit, someone called the cops. Masud, Augie, go back upstairs. I'll handle this," Aboud shouted.

As the police came to a stop in front of the shop, two officers jumped out of the squad car coming to the rescue of the thugs. The two farmers were still pummeling them as they continued to try to get away.

"Okay, boys. That's enough," the officers said, joining the scuffle. They cuffed one then the other with the aid of the two farmers. Everyone had bloody faces and the handcuffed robbers were yelling that they were just passing the house when these two big guys jumped them from nowhere. The officers put the two cuffed men in the car. One pulled the dispatch phone from the dashboard to call in the arrest. The other officer followed Aboud back into the shop to see the damage.

The officer, seeing the destruction, surmised that they were looking for drug money. He asked Aboud to come down to the station in the morning to give an official statement and to fill out the paperwork to press charges. By then the officer said he would know if they were high on drugs and if they had any priors. The squad car pulled away, and Aboud shut the front door.

Masud stepped into the shop, walking around some broken glass. "Well, I guess we learned something. A small shop in a bad neighborhood is a prime target for what happened here tonight. We must assess if this shop idea as a cover for our activities is wise or not. And, Aboud, first thing in the morning, after Augie and I leave, please install motion-detector floodlights on each corner of the house. In fact, Augie, I want you to do the same in New York and Tucson. It's something we should have done in the beginning to thwart anyone sneaking up on us at night, robbers or not. We certainly don't want to bring undo attention to ourselves."

Chapter 32

— • • • —

CATHERINE STOOD STARING out the French doors in her library, arms crossed, waiting for Pete. He called twenty minutes ago saying he was on his way over. He had to talk to her again...privately. She heard Lucy answer the doorbell, exchange greetings, and felt him enter the room.

She turned and looked him in the eye, daring him to say what he had come to say. "It's bad isn't it," she said.

"Catherine, can we sit down?" Pete asked.

She waved her hand indicating for him to take a seat. She remained standing. "How bad is it, Pete?"

"Well, I have to say I was torn as to whether it was a good idea or not to add to your distress, but Hutch, through an intermediary, said he wanted you to know whenever there was a change, a change in the circumstances."

"Oh, sure, through an intermediary. Pete, if this phantom Hutch is real why doesn't he call me?"

"He doesn't think it wise, doesn't want anyone to know of your connection. The woman who took little Stephen has fled, taking him with her."

"Fled? Where did she go?"

"We know where she is but we don't know where she's going. She's—"

"And just how do you know where she is?"

"An agent has her under surveillance."

"Under surveillance, but he can't intercede and rescue Stephen? Is that what you're trying to tell me?"

"Oh, Catherine, it's very complicated—lives are at stake."

"Well, I guess so and one of those lives is my son's. Is there anything else?"

"No, other than I'll call you...you know, if anything changes again." Pete had never felt so uncomfortable in his life. Being stuck in the middle of this struggle, he had no control on either side to help ease the situation.

Catherine walked to her bookcase and picked up a black folder containing some sheets of white paper. She turned, took a few steps to where Pete sat, handing him the document. "Do you recognize this report?"

Pete opened the cover and looked up at Catherine. "Of course, I do. It's the information Tillie typed up about a distributor in Kenya...a supplier of African beads that she's been looking for."

"That's right. It's dated within a week of when Stephen was abducted, and close to the time you first talked to me, when you said you saw Stephen with Hutch. The shop she references in the document is on Amelia Island, Fernandina Beach to be precise. Is that where you saw Stephen? Is it, Pete?" Catherine's eyes never wavered from Pete's face, reading every pulse of blood through his temples.

"Yes. But, Catherine, Hutch is not there now, and the woman has left as well...with Stephen."

"So you say, Pete. So you say. Or are you just trying to steer me away."

—•••—

Catherine's silver BMW sped across the causeway connecting the mainland with Amelia Island. She didn't know what she was going to accomplish by visiting the village of Fernandina Beach. She only knew she was being drawn to the town.

It was just after noon when she pulled into a parking place off Centre Street. With only a cup of coffee for breakfast, she decided the first stop was a deli of some kind to get a sandwich. She spotted a coffee shop with a wooden bench outside. It was next to the street and shaded by a large oak tree. After purchasing a turkey club and a cup of coffee, she settled on the bench, gazing up and down the street as she ate. She tried to picture Hutch with little Stephen window shopping as they walked by the quaint shops.

Finishing her lunch, she tossed her empty coffee cup into a trash receptacle, and crossed the street, heading to the bead shop. She smiled at the life-size pirate, now on the other side of the street, flanking the saloon. *Maybe I'll have a glass of wine before leaving,* she thought. The bead shop was open and again she smiled at the tinkle of the bell on the door—just like Tillie's shop door, she thought.

Catherine introduced herself to the woman behind the counter, who turned out to be the owner. "Do you remember a Tillie Peterson?" Catherine asked. "She stopped in your shop not long ago. She was attracted to your African beads...wanted your distributor's name?"

"Oh, yes. We've corresponded a couple of times by email. In fact, I just received the dealer's latest catalog. Let me show you a new line they're promoting."

The woman pulled out the catalog and thumbed to a page with pictures of the new beads.

"They're lovely, very colorful. Can you give me a copy of this page so I can give it to Tillie?"

"Oh, I wish I could, but my copier is on the fritz. But wait, there's a copy place around the corner. Just let me grab my purse and keys, and I'll go show you. I have a couple of invoices I need to copy. We'll kill two birds with one stone, as they say." The woman chuckled as she led Catherine out of the shop, locking the door behind her.

Chapter 33

— • • • —

MANNY, PRESSING THE pedal to the floor, sped up I-95 heading north to Jacksonville. Peaches sat by his side, nose pointed at the highway, ears up, mouth open, sensing the urgency of her master's driving. Manny heard a sympathetic whine from his pal, but he gave no indication he heard it—no pat on the head. Finally, Peaches curled up on the seat abandoning the notion that danger was imminent.

Manny was following up on a tip that a 2010 Ford Edge, silver gray, vehicle with a plate matching the one from Harry's Bargain Rentals had been turned in a week ago. The owner of the AVIS rental agency didn't remember anything about the man who drove the vehicle in other than it was only one day after the man had rented the car in Georgia. His name was Paul Fisher.

Following the man's directions, Manny pulled off the highway, turned left, and two miles down the road spotted the car rental agency on his right. Parking his squad car in front of the small building, he went in. The interior was clean—gray tile floor, five black-metal chairs, and a desk.

The man behind the desk looked up when Manny walked in. "Hello, Officer. What can I do for you?"

"Hi. Is your name Tom?" The man nodded, yes. "Nice to see you," Manny said extending his hand. "We spoke on the phone this morning. You called about a Ford Edge carrying a Georgia plate. It was turned in last week? Silver, I think you said."

"Oh, yes. Gee, I didn't think you'd drive up here. I don't have the car anymore. It's been rented."

"I understand, but I wanted to ask if you remembered anything about the person who turned it in. You said it was a man?"

"Yes. Nice enough fellow. When I commented that he only rented it for one day, he said it turned out his wife wanted to buy a car."

"I see. Can you describe him?" Manny asked. He pulled up a chair to face Tom, leaning forward, elbows on his thighs—friendly like.

"Not really. I guess he was mid- to late-thirties, black hair."

"Was his wife with him?"

"No. Now that you mention it, he dropped off the car and said he was going to walk a few blocks to meet her. I guess she was at a dealership down the road."

"Did he give you the name of the dealership?"

"No, or at least I didn't pay any attention. A couple more customers needed help."

"Tom, is there a dealership down the road, in walking distance?"

"Yes, there are a couple—a Ford and a Toyota."

—•••—

On a hunch, Manny drove to the Ford dealer. The two rental cars had been Fords, so maybe the guy had a buy-American ad in his head. There didn't seem to be any activity going on and Manny was immediately approached by Harold. His name tag said he was the manager.

"Hello, Officer. How can I help you today?"

"Hello, Harold. My name is Captain Manny Salinas, Daytona Beach PD. I need—"

"Oh, please. Call me Hal," he said shaking Manny's hand.

"Hal, I'm looking for a possible sale you might have had around February 18."

"That shouldn't be too hard to find. I've only sold a few cars in the last couple of months. I'm telling you, if things don't turn around soon, I may have to shut down the business. Let's go to the office. My bookkeeper, Mabel, should be able to tell us right away if there was a sale that day."

Hal led the way to a glassed-in office. A fiftyish woman, salt and pepper hair, wearing a white blouse, sat behind a desk watching the two men come through the door. She was doodling on a calendar blotter. Manny presumed there were no sales to write up.

"Mabel, this officer is looking for a sale we might have had on February 18, give or take a day. Can you check for us?"

"Sure. It shouldn't take me too long—a second or two," Mabel said with a sarcastic smile and a nod to the empty showroom floor.

Hal and Manny were just about to sit down, when Mabel pulled a folder out of the file cabinet. "Would you look at that, only three sales in the past few weeks and one of them was on February 18."

"Do you have a name, anything about who bought it, and, of course, details on the car?" It was all Manny could do not to leap at Mabel and grab the folder from her hands.

"Hal, you remember this one. The man paid cash. When we offered to wash it, vacuum, do an interior scrub down, he said it wouldn't be necessary. He needed it right now. His brother was returning a rental so they had no car."

"Yes, I do remember. Of course, there've been so few sales, that each one is memorable, if you know what I mean," Hal said with a shrug.

"Can you describe the man to me? Hal, you first."

"Sure, late thirties, clean shaven, dark hair, nice guy. While we were writing up the bill-of-sale, his brother came in."

"Oh, what did he look like?"

"Same coloring and about the same age, but his brother had a close-cropped beard, very neat as I recall. He seemed a little nervous—eyes darting around. I remember thinking I wouldn't want to meet him in a dark alley."

"Mabel, is this how you remember them? Anything you want to add?"

"No, except to say I too thought the brother was nervous, a little scary. The car the man bought was one of the nicest we had on the lot—green, 2010, hybrid, Ford Escape, seats five."

"Who bought it?"

"A Mr. Anthony Samuels. He lives in Orlando.

"Mabel, can you make a copy of all the paperwork for the sale? It may be helpful in a case I'm working."

Chapter 34

—•••—

"HEY, FRED, Manny may have turned up a hot lead," Dani said hanging up the phone as she began to attack her computer.

"Where is he?"

"He's on I-95 heading back here from Jacksonville. I hope Peaches has her seatbelt on, because our boss sounded excited."

"What did he say?" Fred asked hitting the save command on his computer and turning to face Dani.

"Later, Fred," Dani quipped, her fingers flying around her keyboard. "I'm tracking down somebody for Manny, an Anthony Samuels who bought a car. He thinks Samuels could have something to do with Catherine's little boy. Let me see what I can find and then we'll talk."

Within seconds Dani had three telephone numbers: A. R. Samuels, A. Samuels, and an Anthony Samuels. Anthony Samuels was out but his wife said she only wished he was thirty-something. He was turning seventy-nine in a month, hard of hearing, and she was tired of shouting. A. R. Samuels, Arnold, asked Dani if she thought he would really be crazy enough to buy a big-ticket item like a car in this economy. A. Samuels, Anthony, was indeed thirty-nine, and definitely did not buy a car in Jacksonville on February 18. However, he did live at thirty-two Klondike, in Orlando.

"Oh, boy. Manny isn't going to be happy about this. On the other hand, maybe he will."

"What do you mean by that?" Fred asked setting a fresh cup of coffee on Dani's desk.

"Looks like he might have turned up another identity theft."

Manny rounded the corner into the bullpen just in time to hear Dani's last two words. "Let me guess," he said. "Anthony Samuels exists, at the address I gave you, in Orlando, but he didn't buy a car?"

"You got it! Ouch. Fred, this coffee is boiling." Dani had taken a short swallow and burned her tongue.

"Fred, put out an APB for a 2010, green, hybrid, Ford Escape," Manny ordered. "Here's the license number. If an officer finds this vehicle, we want to talk to the owner. He would be an immediate person-of-interest. Dani, get the Amber Alert activated again with this new information. Give them the plate and the car make, model and color. I'm calling Cat to let her know we have another lead."

—•••—

Manny reached for his cell, punched the code for Catherine's office number.

"Hi, Maggie. This is Captain Salinas. Is Catherine there?"

"She sure is. Just a sec, I'll put you through."

"Manny, any news?"

"Yes. We have another lead on a car—a green, 2010 Ford Escape, in Jacksonville."

"Oh, I see." Catherine's body immediately became tense. "Georgia and now Jacksonville. What do you think it means?"

"Well, my gut instinct is that we may have stumbled onto some thugs stealing identities is even stronger. Dani called the person on the bill-of-sale. He lives at the address on the paper, but he wasn't in Jacksonville on February 18, and certainly didn't pay cash for a car. Seems he just lost his job."

"Then you don't have anything about my baby? Just some car and a bogus name...a person who didn't buy a car? Manny, you have nothing."

"Cat, don't get upset. We have enough to re-initiate the Amber Alert. I wouldn't call that nothing." Manny was now on his feet, pacing back and forth behind his desk, slamming his chair into the kneehole.

"Manny, I haven't seen my little boy for three weeks. I don't know if he's alive or dead, and you're calling me about a green car," she spit out.

"Cat, I'm sorry. I thought you'd want to hear about this new lead. I'll call you when I know more."

Manny put the receiver back in its cradle. His face was red. He was breathing rapidly as he stared at the phone. "What in the hell was that all about?" he growled under his breath reaching for his Nicorette.

Fred and Dani heard Manny's side of the exchange with Catherine. They looked at each other, eyebrows raised. It didn't sound like the Catherine they knew. What was bothering her?

—•••—

"Pete, it's Catherine."

"Hey, pretty lady. Any news?"

"Don't you give me that pretty lady stuff. I just had a very disturbing phone call from Manny. A call that I should have been pleased to receive. Instead, I'm scared to death...of what? I have no idea. You tell me, Pete." Catherine walked to her office door, pushing it shut, hard.

"What did Manny say?"

"They found another car, or rather information that a car had been purchased," Catherine was practically yelling at Pete. "It's supposed to be the third in a string leading back to the van that the abductors used to get away from the airport. What am I supposed to do, Pete? I should be excited we have a lead. But you're telling me if Manny gets too close to Stephen, or a person you say is Hutch, that they could be in more danger because of some kind of terrorist plot."

"Catherine, I don't know what to tell you. How did you leave it with Manny?"

"Oh, I'm sure he wonders if I've lost my senses. I'm afraid I was abrupt with him and he has no idea why. This new clue is enough to re-initiate the Amber Alert. Pete, we have to tell Manny what's going on. We have to work together. God, help us. My little boy is in the middle of this mess and I can't protect him."

Chapter 35

—•••—

THEY'D BEEN AIRBORNE an hour. With another hour to go, Augie settled into the co-pilot seat and closed his eyes. Their destination was Orange County Airport, a small airport located in Montgomery, New York, about two hours north of New York City. Masud looked at Augie out of the corner of his eye...several times...and finally turned to him. "We're lucky. The clouds are just thick enough to block the full strength of the sun's rays."

Augie opened his eyes and looked out his side window. "Even so, I'm glad I have my sunglasses."

"Rafi told me a little about your skill with the print business, but when I asked him how it was you came to be at the rehab center in El Paso, he wasn't exactly sure, except you couldn't walk when you first arrived."

"I was in a fight and lost," Augie replied.

"Tell me about this fight," Masud asked, with a somewhat piercing glance at Augie.

"It wasn't a very pleasant experience," Augie answered, visualizing how he was going to answer Masud. "I was a freelance reporter for Der Spiegel at the time. Through my job, I was attached to an American Special Forces unit. We were ambushed—most of the squad was wiped out. The few men who survived left me on the side of the road, thinking I was dead."

"Who found you?" Masud asked frowning.

"An army unit quickly came to our rescue. They picked up the few who had left the area and doubled back to check the scene. Thank God for that, because they found me. They airlifted us out of the area on a medical flight to Germany. I was closer to dead than alive. A bullet just missed my heart, but it did something to my spine. I regained consciousness a few days later at the Ramstein Air Base in Germany. After I was stabilized they sent me to a hospital in New York City."

"I believe Layla found you in the rehab center in El Paso. How did you get from New York to El Paso?"

"Mind you, I was paralyzed. Over the next several months, and with hours of physical therapy my body began to heal except for my legs. It was during this time that I became disenchanted with the war, my job, but especially how I was being treated. They weren't giving me the same kind of care as the other patients. I believe it was because I wasn't military. The hospital told me I had to go to a rehab center. They said they'd done all they could and it was up to me to continue a rehabilitation program. When I asked why I couldn't continue the program with them, now get this, the hospital said they had to have the bed for more critically wounded military personnel. I contacted Der Spiegel and got the distinct impression they didn't want to deal with a cripple. I'm sure they just wanted me to die, in other words they abandoned me. They gave me a list of three rehab centers. I chose the one that was as far away from New York as I could get—El Paso, Texas."

"So you're in Texas, paralyzed, then what?" Masud stared out the front windshield of the plane waiting for Augie to reply.

"If it hadn't been for Layla helping me, I might still be confined to that flea-infested bed. She literally took over my rehabilitation. With her strenuous workout routines, I was soon taking a few steps on my own. As I became stronger, my legs got the message and responded. In short order I was walking again, albeit a little unsteady at first. Once I could walk, I had to make a choice—either go back to Germany, where they didn't seem interested in my welfare, or find work here. The rehab center in El Paso also wanted to get rid of me."

"So, you decided to stay in the States."

"Yes. I told Layla I was going to stay in Texas if I could find a job. She asked me what I thought I might do. I told her about my computer experience and my work as a roving photographer. Of course, as a kid I worked for my father. He owned and operated a very high-end print shop in Munich."

"Rather convenient," Masud muttered quietly.

"What do you mean?" Augie asked.

"Never mind. Go on."

"Layla said she would talk to her brother, who was looking for someone with a background similar to mine, but she didn't know if he had already hired someone. Next thing I know, Rafi comes to visit me. His visit was just in time, because the center told me I had to leave by the end of the week. They needed the bed."

"So, Rafi hired you?"

"Sort of. He said I could work for him on a trial basis—three weeks. The thing that sealed the deal for me at the time was that he offered to let me stay in a spare bedroom where he lived. As you know, the room was actually over the print shop he operated."

"Once you started to work for Rafi, when did he share with you what they were actually producing—identity documents?"

"Not right away. Of course, a couple of times, when I saw him giving documents to men who stopped at the shop, I began to suspect what was happening. It must have been at least a month before he approached me. As you know, we were still testing our methods. Then one day a man came into the shop and Rafi asked me to join him in talking to the visitor. It turned out the man was from Pakistan. He had crossed the border into the States two nights before from Juarez, Mexico. I figured it was one of those hand-off deals."

"Hand-off deal?"

"You know. A contact hands you off to a contact, who hands you off, and you end up at a friendly shop. You walk out as an American citizen. Real slick like."

"I see. So you believe in our cause?"

"Masud, I believe in any cause that pays me well. Germany and the U.S. are not at the top of my favorite places. I'm looking to make a lot of money, find myself a place on some island, and live the good life with booze and beautiful women."

Masud's questions ended as he put the jet on a glide path to land at the airport.

Chapter 36

—•••—

LAYLA OPENED her eyes to muted sunlight shining through the sheer curtains in her motel room. Both she and Stephen had fallen into bed exhausted the night before after two long days of travel. But today was a new day, and she was very pleased with her progress. She was now on the west side of Houston, but best of all she knew where she wanted to settle and was eager to hit the road. El Paso was in her sights. She had friends there. Who knows, maybe she can even get her old job back at the Rehabilitation Center.

Stephen was standing in the crib the motel had provided—his thumb in his mouth with his index finger curling over his nose and the other hand holding his blanket up to his face. "You are just too cute for words, my big boy," Layla cooed. "You have been such a good boy that I am officially adopting you. I now dub me as your mommy." Layla gave him a kiss on each pink cheek. "There—real official like."

Turning the television on, she found a cartoon station and positioned the crib so Stephen could watch the Muppets and their antics. Scooting in and out of the shower, she was soon dressed and tended to Stephen's needs.

"Okay, little guy, you and La...mommy are going to get some of that complimentary breakfast and then we'll hit the road." Layla maneuvered the stroller down the long hallway, through the lobby, and into the area filled with the aromas of fresh coffee, pancakes, and muffins. On the way to one of the small tables with a highchair, she swung by the fruit basket and picked up a banana. Reversing direction, back to the table, she popped the baby into the highchair, peeled the banana and broke pieces off into his tray to keep him occupied while she picked up her coffee and a plate of pancakes and scrambled eggs.

After her good night's sleep, a refreshing shower, a hot breakfast, and armed with her new game plan, she was eager to begin her day. Stephen seemed to relish his breakfast as well, swinging his bottle of milk in the air. It slipped out of his hand, hit the rug and rolled under the chair of the table next to them. A man with silver hair smiled and reached down for the bottle.

"Here you go little guy. I think you dropped this. He certainly is a cute baby," the man said to Layla.

"Yes, he is and he's been a good traveler so far."

"I hope he keeps it up. I know when my three were little, it was the devil to pay trying to keep them quiet if my wife wasn't with me. I trust you and your husband take turns driving."

"Oh, my husband isn't with us. He died. But little Stephen and I are doing just fine."

"Well, you certainly are brave striking out on your own. I would think it would be a little scary with no one to check in with."

Layla started to wonder why the man was talking so much. She thought she'd better make it clear that someone was watching out for her, after all she had told Rafi she would call when she finally stopped. "My brother," she said nodding her head in the affirmative, "he gets very upset if I don't talk to him at least twice a day—letting him know exactly where I am, you know."

"That's very wise of him. I'm heading west. Are you going east?"

"No. Me and my little guy are heading west same as you. Well, I guess we'd better be on our way."

"Good luck to you miss...miss?"

"Layla."

"Nice to meet you, Layla. My name is Matt. Maybe we'll bump into each other again...both of us driving west."

Chapter 37

— • • • —

AUGIE WAS SURPRISED at how complete the operation turned out to be! The Montgomery farm was up and running. All he had to do, as far as he could tell at first glance, was to help make the group more efficient, showing them how to turn their harvests into printed documents more quickly. His second surprise was to learn that Masud was the head of the farm. Augie thought for sure he would meet someone new, or that Sayid might be the leader, after all Sayid had greeted them at the airport. He found he had it backwards. Masud was in charge of the New York farm and Sayid was in charge of the Tucson farm. He was informed that Sayid was flying him to Tucson.

Augie was able to show the lieutenant farmers a few new methods of tapping into an individual's personal identification rounding out a resume, a better background story for each set of documents. He was also surprised to discover how many identities the farmers had harvested from the various airports serving the area—Kennedy, LaGuardia, and Newark. The decision by the various credit card companies and the passport officials to embed the RFID chip was obviously being adopted at a rapid rate. *I sure wish people carrying these new cards and passports would protect themselves,* Augie thought. He knew he had to make an opportunity to download the files to his flash drive so he could get the information to the department for processing and surveillance.

While Augie was working with the men, he noticed Masud had many lengthy conversations with Sayid. Several times they mentioned the name of a guy they called Talib. Augie had placed the bugs where he thought JJ could hear their conversations, but more often than not, Masud and Sayid did their planning in the backyard. The cold March weather didn't seem to bother them. They sat at the picnic table in heavy coats, hats, and gloves cradling hot coffee.

The day after they arrived, when Masud and Sayid left the house ostensibly for lunch, Augie stuck a bug under the picnic table, but he couldn't monitor what they were saying because he was never alone. He and JJ set up a rendezvous, by texting, to meet at the high school hockey game. Montgomery Valley Central High only had to win one more game to be able to play in the regional championship event. JJ suggested they meet at the Ice Time Sports Complex, in the snack bar.

— • • • —

The ice arena was mobbed—kids of all ages running, shouting, laughing and eating. It seemed to Augie that every kid either had a hot dog, a chicken-on-a-stick, or a slab of pizza. Many of the little ones had yellow or red stains on their faces from mustard or ketchup, or both. Augie stared at one little boy with the red stuff in his blonde curls. His stomach tightened. An ache permeated his body with longing to hold little Stephen.

"Penny for your thoughts," JJ whispered as he strolled close to Augie but turned in the opposite direction—their backs almost touching. Both men took note that they had their two-way radios. They parted, walking in opposite directions—two strangers listening to music through their earplugs. JJ stayed at the snack bar as almost everyone hurried to their seats. Augie ducked behind the bleachers—the side reserved for Montgomery Valley Central.

The game was about to start. Players from both sides were on the ice facing each other as the referee explained what stick moves would not be tolerated. The teams returned to their boxes leaving the first string players on the ice. The referee blew his whistle, dropped the puck, and the fans immediately screamed their team on.

The agent's radios connected.

"I can't hear you," Augie shouted. "I'm going out front."

"Okay. I'll head to the kid's birthday party I passed coming in. That can't be as noisy as this place," JJ shouted back.

Taking up their new positions, Augie and JJ connected again.

"What's the latest from Matt? Did you hear from Pete? Any news about Catherine?" Augie asked in a rush.

"First, Pete called. He said he told her about the woman fleeing, that being Layla."

"How did she take it?"

"That's what's odd. Pete said he could see her stiffen, determined to solve the situation. She handed Pete a report Tillie had typed up, about African beads and a source on Amelia Island. She confronted him, asking if that's where he saw you and Stephen."

"Oh, shit!"

"It gets better or worse, depending on how you look at it. I heard later in the day from my replacement, Sam Tucker. Catherine evidently drove to Amelia Island and happened to stop in at the Palace Saloon. Sam recognized her from the picture I had given him—one with Stephen and Catherine at his birthday party."

"Did she talk to him or ask any questions?"

"No, just had a glass of wine. She wrote some notes on a pad of paper and left. But, I have one more piece of news. Manny has tracked down the green Ford in Jacksonville, the car Layla took. Catherine called Pete and wants, no, is demanding that they bring Manny in the loop."

"JJ, we have to get this wrap—"

"Shut up, shithead so I can tell you what your Montgomery farmers are scheming," JJ said.

"Okay. Okay."

"About an hour ago, Masud and Sayid were outside—brilliant by the way that you put a bug under the picnic table. They want to get identities mostly for electrical engineers who have experience with power plants. It's my guess that they're going to tamper with the power grid. Remember a few years back when New York City went out and it rippled through other states?"

"I was afraid of this. Some areas were out for days before they found all the transformers that were tripped. If they succeed in putting a major portion of the grid out, they could bring the stock market down, planes would be grounded, and—"

"You got that right," JJ said. "They didn't talk about a timetable other than it wouldn't take long to put their plan in motion once the recruits infiltrated the various power plants. They know where the weaknesses are and how to circumvent the so-called circuit breakers. They also did not mention which plants were on their list. One good bit of news, at least for us, is that they're going to manage both the identity harvest and the recruits from the same houses, at least for now."

"Did you get the impression they already had the recruits in place?" Augie asked. "The house here is big, but there are still only three men."

"Not yet. They were still working on getting the best documents so the power plants would hire them."

"Stop the horse shit, JJ. Where is Stephen and is he safe?"

"Man, you'll never guess what happened this morning. Matt Baker actually talked to Layla while they were having breakfast at a Holiday Inn outside of Houston. He said your son is fine and seems to be happy enough with Layla."

"Did Layla tell Matt where she was going?"

"Not exactly. All Matt could get out of her was that she was heading west. And, get this, he said he was going west, too, and that maybe they would bump into each other again. One more thing, the director was right in that we can't just nab the two of them and bring them in. Layla said her brother expects her to call a few times a day to be sure she's all right. Even if she was blowing smoke, we can't take a chance on jeopardizing the raids. When are you heading to Tucson?"

"With the change in plans, mostly because this farm doesn't need much from me, Sayid said he's flying me to Tucson tomorrow. See if you can find out anything on a man with the first name of Talib. I'll let you know if I get a last name. Then my friend we should be able to throw this net in a coordinated operation— Detroit, New York, Tucson and of course Amelia Island."

"The director has already organized the SWAT teams," JJ said. "The teams are comprised of agents already in the three areas. Amelia Island will be covered from Jacksonville."

"I have one more thing I want you to relay to the director," Augie said. "I have a gut feeling Masud and Sayid are becoming suspicious of me. I mentioned this possibility to the director when we talked, but you and he have to be on the alert. If I ask for instructions to come in, I want them immediately. And, if that happens, Matt has to extract Stephen as well. Do you understand what I'm saying?" Augie's voice rose a little above a whisper as he spit the last words out.

—•••—

Augie always counted on his targets to make a mistake. The only mistake Augie could see so far was that Rafi had hired him. He surmised they did some checking on his background, but it appeared that the story and the documents the director had given him were holding up to scrutiny. However, he knew he had to be on guard, always alert to the possibility that his cover was blown.

On his way back to the farmhouse, Augie decided to send one more text message to Rafi.

> "have u heard from layla?"
>
> "yes," Rafi replied.
>
> "did she say baby okay?" Augie waited anxiously for the reply.
>
> "not from layla, but baby mom stopped in shop yesterday. a bead lady down the block brought her 2 make copies."
>
> "trouble?" Augie asked
>
> "doubtful. just coincidence. glad kid wasn't here." Rafi replied.

—•••—

Masud answered the phone and heard Rafi on the other end of the line.

"Masud, I wanted to let you know that Pasha and I came up with two electrical engineers in our last harvest at the Jacksonville Airport. In checking their backgrounds, both had worked at a power plant but are now working as contractors out of the country."

"That is good news, Rafi. Send the files to me and we'll prepare the documents here in Montgomery. Have you heard from Layla yet?"

Chuckling Rafi answered, "Not yet. You are the second person in the last hour to ask me if I'd heard from her."

"Oh. Who else asked about her?"

"Augie. He sent me a text message asking about her and the little boy. He became quite attached to the baby before he left to go to Detroit."

Chapter 38

—•••—

"CAT, I APPRECIATE your inviting me to attend the meeting with the reporter. The last time we talked on the phone I had the feeling something was wrong. Was there? Was there something you didn't want to share with me?" Manny asked.

"No. I'm afraid it was just one of those days where I was losing it. Not knowing where my baby is, or even if he's okay, is beyond terrifying. Thank you for being here to see what the reporter's angle is."

"What did he tell you when he called? What publication does he represent?"

"He didn't really say. He inferred that the story would be local, but that it might get picked up by the AP and—"

"Well, hello there, pretty lady. Lucy let me in. She caught me before I had a chance to ring the bell. She said I'd find you in the library," Pete said throwing a smile to Catherine. "Manny, good to see you." The men shook hands and Pete sat down on the straight-back chair facing the couch. Peaches pranced up to Pete, obviously one of her favorite friends, putting her paw up on his knee. She was rewarded with a scratch behind her ears. "Yes, yes, you're a nice dog. Look what I have for you." Pete pulled out a medium-sized dog biscuit which Peaches carefully removed from his fingers. Prancing over to the edge of the red Oriental rug and laying down, she licked the biscuit a few times before biting off an end.

Manny had a perplexed look on his face. "Cat, I wasn't aware Pete was joining the interview. Is there anyone else coming?"

Catherine looked from Pete to Manny and shook her head no. The tension in the room was palpable but eased slightly when Lucy brought in a coffee service, setting it on the butler's table in front of the leather couch. "Thank you, Lucy. Please show Mr. Whitehead in when he arrives."

Manny looked down at the tray which held a service for four. He looked from Catherine to Pete. The doorbell rang in the background and the three in the library braced for the reporter.

"Miss Catherine, this is Mr. Whitehead. He said you were expecting him."

"Yes. Won't you come in, Mr. Whitehead? I'd like you to meet Captain Manny Salinas, and my friend Pete Peterson."

"Thank you, Mrs. Hainsworth. Gentlemen," Mr. Whitehead shook hands all around.

"Won't you have a seat, Mr. Whitehead?" Catherine motioned to a chair next to Pete, and she and Manny sat on the couch.

"Please, call me Paul. As I said on the phone, I'm here to do a human interest story on the abduction of your son. I've read all the articles I could find, and have heard a few news broadcasts about the Amber Alert, and your interviews, Mrs. Hainsworth. Before writing the piece I wanted to meet you and to see if there was anything new to report."

"Excuse me, Mr. Whitehead, Paul, do you have some identification?" Manny asked.

"Of course," Mr. Whitehead said, pulling out his wallet and a reporter's AP badge. "Mrs. Hainsworth asked me to bring some identification."

"I thought you said you were local," Pete said taking the badge that Manny passed to Catherine, and she to Pete. "This is for AP— you thought they might pick it up?"

"Yes, my stories tend to be about this area, but if it has a wider interest, then I submit them to the AP."

Manny spoke up. "If you've read the bulletins you know about the two cars we believe are linked to the getaway van."

"Yes. Have there been any new developments?"

"Not as yet, but we're hoping," Catherine said.

"I see a picture of you, Mrs. Hainsworth, with a gentleman. Is that the boy's father?" Mr. Whitehead asked.

Catherine followed the man's gaze to her cherished picture taken of her and Hutch. The only picture she had of him. "No. No it isn't. That's a picture of my brother and me."

"I see. Your brother is nice looking." Whitehead went over and picked up the picture. Setting it down, he said, "Well, if there isn't any more news, I guess I'll go with what I have. Thank you for your time."

Manny walked Whitehead to the front door. "I hope Mrs. Hainsworth's son is found soon. Thank you for your time, Captain Salinas."

Manny and Peaches went back to the library. Catherine and Pete looked at him, neither saying a word. "I don't know about you, Pete, but I didn't like that guy," Manny said. "He also seemed to be in a hurry to leave."

"Manny, I think he was okay. After all, we didn't have anything new to give him," Catherine said.

"Cat, why did you lie about the picture of you and Hutch? I really feel you're holding back on me. You know I'm trying to help you find Stephen."

"Manny, don't be ridiculous. I asked you to be with me when Mr. Whitehead came for the interview. I don't know why I lied. It just popped out of my mouth. Please don't make this harder than it already is." Catherine stood and started to walk out of the library giving him the distinct indication that the event was over and she would escort him to the door.

Manny sighed, shook his head, and said goodbye to Pete. At the door he turned back to face Catherine and caught a sympathetic look in her eyes as she closed the door after him.

Walking back into the library, Catherine caught Pete with his head bowed, deep in thought.

"So, what did you think of Mr. Whitehead?" she asked Pete.

"I smell a rat. He was no more a reporter than I am the next Boston Marathon winner. I suggest you don't give any more interviews for awhile."

"No more press conferences? No more asking the public to help? Manny won't buy it. Pete, I can't treat him this way. We've always been open with each other. I know he thinks I'm lying when I say I'm not holding back."

"Yep, I could see it written on his face. My problem is I don't know if he'll play ball with the feds or will he insist on pursuing the case on his own. His way."

"The case? Pete this is more than a case. This is my baby we're talking about." Catherine, no longer able to control her anger, her frustration, or her fears, lashed at the person in front of her. "You say Hutch is watching out for him. How in God's name are you so sure he's alive? Maybe the person you saw was someone else. He just looked like Hutch. I'll tell you one thing, Mr. Peterson, if you don't give me a good reason in the next twenty-four hours, if you don't give me compelling evidence that what you say is true, I'm going to tell Manny everything you've told me."

Chapter 39

—•••—

MONTGOMERY WON THEIR semi-final hockey game and was now in the playoff. The anticipation that their team would win, saw many families in Montgomery preparing for the ten-mile trek to the ice arena in Newburgh. It didn't seem to matter if they had children in high school or not, they weren't going to miss the championship game.

Again the crowd noise bounced off the wall—the air filled with laughter, shrieks from friends greeting friends, and the constant calling for one child or another to come back to the parent in charge. The high school bands marched through the arena, queuing up to play the Star Spangled Banner as the flag was raised. Parents sang and watched with pride, and the spectators smiled in appreciation. The area was cleared, the puck dropped, and the battle began.

Augie and JJ, once again unable to hear, moved out of the ice arena to a quiet area of the sports complex. JJ stood outside the pro shop and Augie retreated to a corner with chairs reserved for people who just wanted to sit and wait for their friends. At this time the seats were unoccupied—everyone was watching the beginning of the game.

The radios connected. "You're sure this is a good idea?" Augie asked.

"We're so close to closing this evil group down, we can't take a chance that a local cop in Daytona Beach could blow the whole operation," JJ replied. "Pete is with Catherine. He'll pick up the phone to be sure it's you and then hand it to her. Are you okay?"

"JJ, I feel like a kid about to kiss his first date. I can't wait, but I'm scared she'll tell me to buzz off."

"Fat chance of that happening. Well, good luck, buddy." Augie dug out his cell phone, punched the numbers, and lifted the phone to his ear.

"Hutch, is that you?" Pete asked, knowing it was but trying to give Catherine time to prepare herself.

"The one and only, you shithead. When I hang up please take care of her...will you? Promise me."

"I promise. Here's Catherine."

"Hello, whoever you are. Just to let you know you can't fool me. I know Hutch's voice!" Catherine said angrily into the mouthpiece.

Hutch closed his eyes, swallowed hard, his pulse raced at the sound of her voice. "Hi, beautiful, it's me."

Catherine gasped for air. She sank down into the downy cushions of the couch holding the phone with both hands for fear one would let go of the instrument. "Hutch," she whispered, "it is you. How...why didn't you tell me...you were alive. I would have...I would have stayed by your side...no matter how bad."

"I know you would have and that's why I stupidly made everyone swear to leave it that I had died. Catherine, my dear sweet love, I was as good as dead...believe me. But, when I saw you in such pain talking about your baby...God, Catherine...our baby, I knew I'd made a mistake. Since that moment every breath I've taken has been to find a way to return to you. Do you believe me? Catherine, I love you with all my heart."

"My darling, I believe you. When will you and our baby come home to me?"

"Soon, sweetheart...very soon."

Chapter 40

—•••—

THE FLASHING NEON sign, "Vacancy," beckoned to Layla. She pulled into the parking spot closest to the lobby. Exhausted from over ten hours on the road, she turned the ignition key off, leaned her head back, closed her eyes, and breathed a heavy sigh.

"We made it, Stephen. We're in El Paso. You've been such a little trooper today. Mommy never could have done it without your help. Now be a good boy for a few more minutes while I register for a room."

After locking the car doors, she walked into the lobby, taking note of the McDonalds across the street and a gas station on the corner. The motel attendant said she would have a crib set up in her room shortly. Layla thought that this would be a good time to get a sandwich. By the time they finished eating their room with the crib would be ready. Layla was almost in tears with the kindness everyone showed her and the baby. She slowly ate her fish burger while Stephen, eating the bits of a bun and some applesauce, was kept amused by an elderly couple sitting at a table across from them.

When Layla opened the door to her room, the crib was set up and the covers on her bed were turned down. Changing Stephen into his jammies, she popped him into bed. He fell asleep the minute she laid him in the crib. It was now eight o'clock. Ten o'clock on the east coast. "I guess it's time to call Rafi," she said to herself, punching in his number on her cell.

"Layla, where the hell are you? I've been worried sick about you, and Masud and Sayid aren't happy you took off without telling us where you were going."

"Oh, Rafi, stop shouting. I've had a hard few days but I'm finally home."

"Home? What do you mean home?"

"El Paso, silly. When I left Amelia Island, I wasn't sure where I was going. I just wanted to get away. And, don't give me that business that Masud or Sayid cared about me. I'm sure they said good riddance to me and the baby."

"Okay, well, *I* was worried. What are you going to do? And what are you doing for money?"

"When I left Houston this morning—actually I was already through the worst part—I stopped at a couple of ATM's and used a few of the cards you gave me. I have several thousand dollars in cash which should do me until I get a job."

"A job? Come on, Layla, you're here illegally so that could be risky."

"Excuse me, Mr. Smarty Pants, I have the documents proving I'm a U.S. citizen from when we were living in El Paso, before you uprooted the farm and moved us to Florida."

"Where are you now?"

"I'm in a motel. Stephen and I just had dinner and we're both going to sleep 'til noon. We're very tired from all that driving. Then I'm going to look for a small furnished apartment. Once we settle in, I'll try to get my old job back at the rehabilitation center."

"You seem to have everything planned out. Does this mean you'll now answer my phone calls?"

"Yes, dear brother, I will. How are you? Anything new at the farm?"

"Some big things are going to happen soon, Layla. It's probably just as well you aren't here. I don't have time to go into it now because I'm in the middle of a crucial background search. I may have some information for you in the morning, so please keep your cell charged."

Chapter 41

— • • • —

THE SMALL JET cut through the night sky at record speed. Sayid was eager to return to his Tucson farm. However, his thoughts were not the training Augie was to give the farm, but on his meeting with Talib, the Al Qaida leader in charge of the next strike—perhaps Memorial Day but no later than the fourth of July. *Stupid American's and their predilection to name everything,* he thought. *But Talib picked a perfect name—Operation Hyena—a dog-like animal with a howl that sounds like human laughter. Well, Talib and the farmers would be the ones doing the laughing after the operation.* Oh, how he relished the thought of that celebration.

"What's so funny, Sayid?" Augie asked.

"You'll know soon enough, my friend. You'll know soon enough."

A chill ran down Augie's back. Was the devil himself flying the plane?

— • • • —

One of Tucson's lieutenant farmers picked up Sayid and Augie at a small airport outside of the city limits. The three talked about the hot spring weather on the desert as they drove the twenty-five miles to the farmhouse. The house was located in a run-down neighborhood much like the location of the El Paso farm building. It was a southern style ranch, built of concrete block. A screened in patio on the north side was a delightful place to sit except in the heat of summer. The patio was a nice retreat but the view was of a weed-infested lawn, a partially broken wood fence beyond which shielded an alley for garbage pickup. This house and the one in Detroit could have been side-by-side in the same neighborhood.

Augie took over a bedroom on the second floor and the first thing he did was to text JJ with his location and other logistics.

"ask director if raid ready day after tomorrow."

"ok," JJ replied.

"all farms except amelia island now protected with spotlights."

"where spots?" JJ asked.

"2 each corner of building."

"okay, can u flip switch here?" JJ asked.

"yes, swat must deal with other locals. stephen?"

"layla still heading west."

"matt?" Augie asked.

"on her tail."

"will text any new info later today. bye."

"bye." JJ replied.

— ••• —

"What are you saying, Rafi? Masud thinks there is more to Augie's interest in the little boy than he's letting on?" Sayid walked outside and on through a broken gate in the backyard to the road. He needed privacy. There was a slight smell of garbage rotting in the Arizona sun.

"Yes," Rafi replied. "Augie sent me a text message asking if I had heard from Layla and was the baby okay. Anyway, the message caused a little bell to go off in Masud's head. He asked me to pay a visit to the woman, a Catherine Hainsworth, the mother of the baby Layla abducted. She's been in the news giving press conferences. I was busy preparing some documents from a recent harvest, so Pasha went in my place. He pretended he was a reporter seeking information for a human interest story. He used the name of Paul Whitehead and took reporter's credentials."

"Did he see the woman?" Sayid asked.

"Yes, and the police captain who is working the case. There was another man as well, a Mr. Peterson."

"Come on, Rafi. Nothing you've said tells me anything unusual about Augie. You're wasting my time. I have the leader of Operation Hyena coming in an hour and you're rattling on about Pasha playing like a reporter."

"Well, listen to this. While in her house, Pasha saw a picture of the woman with a man."

"So?" Sayid rolled his eyes, shook his head and headed back to the house.

"So, Pasha is almost certain the man in the picture was Augie without the long ratty hair."

"I see." Sayid stopped in his tracks, his face white—blood draining away from shock, eyes narrow slits—as his mind processed the possibility that Augie was a mole.

"Have you talked with Masud about Pasha's observation?"

"Yes. We're both researching Augie's background. Everything we've come up so far seems to indicate that Augie is who he says he is—Augustoff Weiss from Germany, born of German parents."

"Well, let me know if you find something on our friend that corroborates your suspicions. I must go now to meet Talib."

—•••—

The Tucson farm was ready for training. The only items lacking were printing supplies. They had followed Augie's instructions down to the last period. The lieutenant farmer, reporting to Sayid, had introduced himself to the supplier Augie had given him. The lieutenant didn't place the order, preferring to wait for Augie to be sure the first purchase was correct. Augie suggested they go immediately to the dealer so he could begin showing them the production process. While the lieutenant went in search of Sayid, to let him know where they were going, Augie placed several bugs—one in the workroom, the kitchen, and the small shop area in the front of the house. He wasn't sure if Sayid was going to include him in the discussions with the man he was expecting, but he knew it was a significant meeting.

Augie and the lieutenant took the farm's van to the dealer. The supplier had already filled the items on the list that Augie emailed him the week before. Everything was assembled on the loading dock in back of his building. Checking the list of items, Augie added a couple of additional packages of the special paper as well as more ink cartridges. The transaction was completed in cash. There was no bill-of-sale.

Chapter 42

—•••—

"JJ, PETE HERE. We have a situation brewing that you need to be aware of. In fact, I have a couple of things to relay to you."

"Go ahead, Pete. Whatcha got?"

"First, a reporter came to interview Catherine today about the abduction of her baby. He said he wanted to talk to her because he was writing a human interest story."

"So, go on."

"He was as phony as a snake hiding in an armadillo shell."

"How so?"

"He seemed nervous, twitchy like, kept looking around the room. We were in Catherine's library."

"Who's we?"

"Catherine, Manny, who is another problem, and me. Anyway this guy, Paul Whitehead, spots a picture of Catherine and Hutch on the end table. He walks over, picks it up, and asks if this was a picture of the baby's father."

"What did she say?"

"For some unknown reason, even she can't explain, she told him no. Catherine said it was a picture of her brother, one of the last ones with the two of them together before he was killed."

"Did he buy it?"

"I'm not sure."

"What did the guy look like?"

"That's another thing, he looked Middle Eastern, you know, olive skin, black hair, and he had a black beard, clipped short."

"Shit."

"What? Do you recognize the description?"

"I think so. You said you had a couple of situations. What else?"

"Well, Catherine is just about at her wits end. In her heart, she wants to believe me that I saw Hutch and her baby, but her mind says otherwise. Manny asked questions after the reporter left. Questions Catherine didn't answer. So they had a bit of a tiff and she escorted Manny out of the house. Then she turns to me and says that in twenty-four hours she's going to tell Manny everything I've told her unless I give her a good solid reason, a believable reason, why she shouldn't."

"What did she mean by that?"

"I don't know, because there isn't anything but the cars, which keep coming up with owners who couldn't be owners. If you know what I mean. Shit, I don't even know what I mean. I think she keeps thinking about Hutch getting killed at the end of the last mission. And now finding him alive, maybe this time he won't be so lucky, which leaves her baby in the middle of the mess with no protection."

"Pete, you have to keep stalling. I'm going to talk to Hutch because from what you say about the reporter, I think he's been burned. All I can tell you is that I think it will be over in the next twenty-four hours so you don't have to worry about Catherine, other than trying to ease her mind."

"And how do you expect me to do that?"

Chapter 43

— • • • —

LAYLA WAS LUCKY. She found a furnished apartment with a garage. The owner of the building was very happy she came along because her previous tenant had skipped town without paying the last month's rent. To top it off, the landlady had grandchildren so she was more than happy to loan Layla a crib and a highchair until she was able to buy her own.

It was early afternoon and even though she was tired she decided to make a run to the laundromat down the street. She tucked Stephen in the crib. He always took a long afternoon nap, so she felt she had plenty of time to do at least two loads. Besides she was just going down the street. Dumping all their dirty clothes into two large bags she headed into the garage. She backed out, closed the garage door behind her with the remote the landlady had given her with the apartment, and headed down the street.

The laundromat wasn't busy and given the large washing machines, she was pretty sure she could wash all of their clothes before Stephen woke up. Unbeknownst to Layla, her faithful companion, Matt, was parked across the street and down a few store fronts. He had been joined by a second agent, Scott Fitzwilliam—more force to help when he moved in on Layla and the baby.

It had taken almost two hours to finish up the laundry, but she still made a quick stop at the drugstore for a supply of diapers, a newspaper, and a new tube of lip gloss. Turning into her driveway, she pulled out the garage door opener as if it were her new toy. Parking the car in the garage, she then grabbed her bags of clean clothes and headed into the apartment. Stepping into the kitchen she turned to shut the door.

"It's about time you came home," Rafi said.

Startled, Layla dropped the bags and swung around to face her brother. "Rafi, for God sake you scared the daylights out of me. What are you doing here and how did you get in?"

"Come on, dear sister, you're still up to your old tricks. You left the front door unlocked."

"Oh, my God. I don't believe I could have done such a thing and leaving Stephen here alone." She hurried down the hall.

"Don't run. He's not there."

Layla opened the door to the bedroom she was going to set up for the baby. The crib was empty. Racing back to the kitchen, she yelled, "What have you done with him. If you hurt him, I swear I'll kill you."

"Calm down, Layla. Yes, I took him. We had to get rid of him. I put the baby in good hands. Now listen to me. I have some things to tell you and then we have to get out of here."

"I won't listen. What have you done to my baby?" She was in Rafi's face, pounding his chest, tears flowing down her cheeks.

Rafi took her by the shoulders and forcibly sat her down on a kitchen chair. "Layla, shut up and listen to me. We're in danger of being picked up by the cops, or the feds, or I don't know who else. And, all because you nabbed that stupid kid."

"What are you saying? We're going to be arrested?" Rafi now had her full attention as she wiped the tears away with the back of her hands.

"Actually, I don't know for sure yet, but Pasha posed as a reporter and went to interview the baby's mother."

"Why did he do that, for heaven sake?"

"Augie called a few times inquiring about you?"

"He did? Maybe he wants me after all."

"Sure, he wants you all right. Behind bars. Each time he called he particularly inquired about the baby, hoping he was okay, and had you called to say where you had taken him. So talking to

Masud about these calls one day, Masud said he was getting a feeling about Augie."

"A feeling? What kind of feeling?"

"That maybe he wasn't who he said he was. With his interest in the baby, we started to wonder if there was a connection. That's when Pasha went to see his mother. While he was in her house, he saw a picture of her with a man. Pasha asked if this was the baby's father. The woman denied it, but Pasha got the distinct impression that she was lying."

Layla's eyes grew wide. You think that Augie is Stephen's father?"

"We don't know yet, but Masud is digging into his background. I didn't wait to hear the results. I knew you had to dump the kid and I was afraid you wouldn't do it. So I hopped a flight. When I called you this morning to get your address, I was already in El Paso. I saw you leave without Stephen, so I took a chance you'd put him down for his afternoon nap. Now you know everything."

"But you still don't have proof that Augie is spying on us. There's still a chance he wants to be with me." Layla sat down on a kitchen chair and stared at her brother, her face stained with tears.

"Don't kid yourself, Layla. If Augie is really not sympathetic to our cause, then that means he, or someone he is passing information to, is monitoring the farms and could move in on us at any time. I suggest you pack a small suitcase, with just enough to see you through a couple of nights. We're going to ditch your car and get out of El Paso. While you're throwing your stuff together, be sure to take any identification and credit cards you've been using, I'm going to call Masud to see if he's come up with anything yet. Now, hurry up."

It took Layla only a few minutes to pack her overnight bag. Looking in one last time at the empty crib, she again felt a pang in her stomach to hold her baby again. She didn't even have a chance to kiss him goodbye. Rafi closed his cell as she joined him in the kitchen.

"Any information from Masud?"

"Nothing yet."

"Maybe Augie is one of us. Maybe he wants me and the baby...to be a family...and you—"

"Forget it, Layla. Come on get in the car and let's get out of here."

—•••—

"Matt, look. The garage door is opening again," Scottie said pointing out the window at the garage door located down a few buildings.

"I see. I see," Matt said. "What I don't see is that big car seat in the back. Maybe I'm blind—do you see it?"

"No, I don't. Hold it. A man's driving the car and Layla's sitting in the passenger seat."

"Scottie, did the team give you pictures of the Amelia Island farmers?"

"Yah...Rafi and Pasha. Just a sec...let me dig them out of my pocket."

Layla's car squealed away from the curb and merged into the afternoon traffic. Matt pulled out and took his position a few cars behind. "If I'm not mistaken," Matt said, "the driver of that car is Layla's brother. The way he took off makes me think they're trying to make a get away, but shit we didn't see the baby."

"Maybe he's laying down in the backseat." Scottie took another look at the two men in the picture and then stuffed it back in his pocket.

"Doubtful. Layla may be wanted for kidnapping, but she's not likely to hurt that baby. In her mind, she's now his mother. I say we watch for an opportunity to move in and arrest them. However, we can't let them sound an alarm or communicate in any way with their farmer friends."

Once the car squealed away from Layla's apartment, the man kept to the speed limit. The car danced in and out of the light traffic and then turned into a Wal-Mart parking lot. The man headed to an empty parking spot but the area was packed with cars. Layla and the man got out of the car, and he pulled her suitcase out of the backseat.

"That's him. That's Layla's brother Rafi. Scottie, they're ditching that car. Come on, partner. It's arrest time."

Matt and Scottie walked up behind Layla and Rafi, and with a swift karate chop Scottie took control of Rafi, flinging him against the side of a parked car. Matt quickly slammed Layla against the car parked next to the sedan where Scottie was cuffing Rafi and slapped a pair of cuffs around her wrists. Matt turned Layla around and with his big hands pinned her shoulders to the car.

"Where's the baby, Layla? Where is he?" he said hissing into her face.

"You...you...I don't know. I—"

"Stop looking at your brother. Where's the baby?" Matt's face was only inches from her. The grandfatherly looking man had turned into a no-nonsense officer as he continued to pin her against the trunk of the car.

"What baby?" Rafi yelled back. "We don't know what you're talking about. Who are you?"

"None of your business who we are. As far as not knowing what we're talking about, well, we'll just see about that," Matt yelled back.

Scottie grabbed Layla's suitcase with one hand, and in a vice-like grip propelled Rafi to Matt's car. As Matt yanked Layla forward, he paused beside her car, checking to see if by any chance Stephen was inside. "Hey, Scottie, get the car keys from that bastard so we can pop the backend. Let's be sure the kid isn't inside."

Checking the car, and pocketing the garage opener, they were satisfied it was empty. "Okay, you two, we're going back to Miss Layla's little apartment. We're going to have a nice face-to-face chat about a certain child, and where that child might be."

Back at the apartment, Matt pulled his black SUV into the garage and shut the door. "I think we'll separate these two, Scottie. Let me sit the little mother in the kitchen with leg bracelets as well as her handcuffs. You take big brother into the living room. There must be a nice chair in there you can tie him to. There's some Duct tape under the front seat of the car. Seal his mouth so he doesn't get any ideas about calling for help. On the other hand, he probably doesn't want to see the cops either, and we certainly wouldn't want them butting into our fun, now would we?"

"Okay, Layla, where's the baby?" Matt asked standing in front of her as he cuffed her ankles together.

"I don't know, and if I did I wouldn't tell you," she said tears streaming down her face.

"If I turn you over to the police, you'll be facing serious jail time for kidnapping a baby. On the other hand, if I take him off your hands, you'll be off the hook. Now where is he? Did your brother take him?"

"I told you, I don't know where he is. I didn't even know my brother was in town, and who are you anyway?" She was now sobbing uncontrollably, gasping for air. Matt put a piece of tape over her mouth and went to see if Scottie was having any luck. Rafi's mouth was shut tight. He had evidently decided silence was the best thing. Scottie was slapping a piece of tape over Rafi's clenched lips just in case he decided to cry out for help.

With Rafi and Layla secured, Matt went out to the garage and called the director to apprise him of the situation. He told the director they had no choice but to move in. "We have them on ice, sir, so they can't send out any messages to alert the farms that they've been taken prisoner. Scottie and I are assuming the roles of random outlaws."

"What about the baby?" the director asked.

"We're working on it," was all Matt could reply.

Chapter 44

— • • • —

A GHOSTLY SHIMMER outlined the silver plane in the light of the full moon. Landing on the un-towered airfield, the pilot taxied to an open hangar and cut the engine. A car, headlights on low beam, slowly approached the plane as the pilot stepped down onto the tarmac. The car came to a stop. The pilot opened the passenger door and slid into the vehicle.

"Talib, good to see you my friend," Sayid said sitting next to the man in the back seat. The driver turned the car around and headed out to the rutty, dirt road.

"Cell phones, text messages, email—they cannot replace face-to-face communication when missions with the magnitude of ours go live. There is no room for misunderstandings," Talib said. He fastened his seatbelt, and let out a sigh as he leaned back to relax.

"Did you have a hard trip, Talib?" Sayid asked.

"Not really. It was long but uneventful. I wanted to see your operation before launching the recruiting effort."

"Everyone will be asleep when we reach the farm, so we'll have complete privacy. It's a little chilly on the desert tonight, so I'll put on a pot of coffee. You'll be comfortable in the kitchen?"

"Yes, yes, the kitchen is fine."

Fifteen minutes later, the lieutenant pulled the car into the driveway and the two men went into the house. Sayid put Talib's suitcase in the extra first-floor bedroom and then went into the kitchen to start the coffee.

Talib joined him, the aroma of the coffee pulling him into the kitchen. "I just took a look at the workshop. Very impressive, Sayid."

"Yes, Augie has done a masterful job making the farms operational. You'll meet him in the morning. Now, tell me your plans, dear friend. How far along are you?"

"I have the top recruits in WMD assigned but not in this country as yet. Of course, that is the main reason I traveled here to see the farms for myself. I will give you a list of identification documents I will need before I leave you, which will be the day after tomorrow. I think we'll have finished our planning by then, don't you?"

"That is your call, Talib. Only you know what we have to discuss. My timetable is your timetable. Ah, would you like a little more coffee?"

"Yes, please."

"Tell me more about the backgrounds your people will need. I want to get you the very best so they will have no trouble finding jobs at the various facilities you plan to hit."

"Mostly top engineers and scientists in chemical, biological, and of course electrical disciplines. Although, a mid-level engineer may have an easier time landing a job. Of course, he will know what he's looking for so all he has to do is infiltrate the plant. I'm thinking, Sayid, that we should expand our farms. Closer to more ports and points of entry, say Seattle, San Francisco, San Diego, and Miami."

"So many, Talib? Sounds as if you plan to bring in an army," Sayid chuckled.

"Precisely, my friend. Over the next five years, the mission will require several hundred dossiers, maybe a thousand. As you know I have named this major battle plan Operation Hyena, the scavenger dog. By the time the stupid Americans catch on to what we have done, it will be too late. The infrastructure—water, power grid, transportation—will be severely weakened The U.S. population will be paralyzed with fear not knowing where or how the next strike will occur."

"That will be a most triumphant moment, Talib."

Chapter 45

— • • • —

THE TUCSON FARMHOUSE was quiet. It was well after midnight before Talib and Sayid said goodnight to each other, slipping into their respective rooms. Talib said he was only staying one day, and would be leaving the following morning.

It was now 2:15 a.m. Augie had waited for over an hour after the lights were switched off to send his messages. He scrunched down under the covers of his bed and began texting JJ and the director.

"big man, talib, leaves in 24 hours."

"idea who he is?" the director asked.

"my gut says al qaida."

"i figured."

"prep swat 4 all farms plus rescue stephen." Augie ordered.

"ok." JJ answered.

"coordinate raids same time—no alarms must be sent out." Augie continued.

"when?" JJ asked.

"tomorrow night before players scramble."

The director replied: "confirmed. net will be thrown at 2:45 am est. tomorrow night."

JJ typed: "there is a problem."

"what?" Augie asked.

"pasha posed as reporter."

"and?" Augie asked.

"he may have ID'd you from pic on table."

"when?" Augie asked.

"this morning. could get dicey your end. are u armed?"

"yes."

JJ continued: "rafi joined layla in el paso. matt has both on ice."

"stephen?" Augie asked.

"stephen missing." JJ replied.

"What the hell," Augie said to himself as he bolted from bed. Augie replied: "FIND HIM!"

JJ replied: "WE WILL! no indication he's harmed."

—•••—

It was past seven o'clock in the morning before Talib and Sayid came into the kitchen for breakfast. Hoping to rouse the two, Augie put on a fresh pot of coffee. The gurgling of the automatic pot did the trick. As was the farmers' custom, each fixed their own breakfast, with the exception of this day—Sayid catered to Talib. It had been different when Layla was around. She enjoyed making a big deal out of the first meal of the day. Today they were on their own.

"Augie, I've admired how quickly you bring the farms up to speed," Talib said. "From the reports I've received, they are ahead in the harvest. This is mainly due to your efforts—your training, your preparation, and your patience with those not so quick to grasp what you were trying to show them. We have now come to the culmination of these efforts. Our recruits will start pouring over the borders. As I told Sayid last night, it seems to make sense to open two or three more farms so the recruits can more quickly get their papers."

"Where and when do you want to make these new farms operational?" Augie asked. He had to remain calm, to pay close attention to the mission at hand so he didn't trip up. But, his thoughts kept returning to the little boy with blonde curls.

"Immediately," Sayid said.

"I think Seattle, San Diego, and Miami for starters," Talib said. "Also, to keep the recruit's spirits up and keep them focused, we want one of the established farms to pull off, shall we say, an appetizer."

"An appetizer?" Augie asked.

"Yes, something like what the Americans call *getting your feet wet*."

"Sounds interesting. Just how will they get their feet wet?" Augie asked.

"You will soon see, my friend. Maybe Memorial Day," Talib replied. "Yes, I have the plans for a little Memorial Day celebration. I'm meeting with Masud and a couple of his farm hands when I leave here. We can easily pull off a mission in New York. Then we have something to show potential recruits. Your Nazi brothers will be proud of you, Augie. I dare say they would wish to be in your place, to pull off the initial celebration, which in time will lead to the biggest events ever seen in the western world."

Chapter 46

—•••—

EXCITED BY THEIR APPARENT success, two farmers headed back to the Montgomery farmhouse from JFK airport. They chatted about their scans—prospects they had passed, bumped into, or stood in line with while waiting to go through security. Once they were within reach of the ticket counter, with only five or so people in front of them, they would swear to themselves that they had forgotten something and leave the line. The people around them, holding out their passports or other photo IDs, just moved ahead to fill the vacated space.

Several times during the day, while his men were at the airport and the house was quiet, Masud thought he would be able to get back to his computer to perform more searches into the background of Augustoff Weiss. He tried early in the morning and then again throughout the afternoon, but problems of one sort or another kept him away from his computer. Then the downloading of the new scanned files from the farmers seemed especially slow, or the software generated error messages stating the files were unreadable. Everyone seemed on edge. For some reason, the printers were jamming and the new documents were coming out blurry. At six o'clock, Masud put a stop to the madness, shut down the equipment, and everyone went to a small local restaurant down the street for dinner and a drink. Tomorrow they would start fresh.

By the time the group returned from dinner, and finished hashing over the day's software glitches, it was almost midnight. Masud was tired but he decided to perform one last search for more information on Augie's background. So far everything coincided with what he had told Layla when she met him at the rehabilitation center in El Paso, as well as later when Rafi talked to him about his experience as a printer. Masud had sent an email the day before to a friend in Germany, Munich to be specific. So far there had been no reply.

For over another hour, Masud tried pursuing many different links, some he had used before when researching a person's background, even some new ones Augie had shown him. He took his glasses off, rubbed his eyes, and padded down the hallway for a beer. "Then I'll go to bed," he told himself.

Chapter 47

—••••—

CATHERINE'S HOUSE WAS quiet even though her close friends and confidants were all there. The vigil had begun. Pete felt the SWAT raids would begin sometime in the next few hours. He was not told exactly what time.

Lucy had prepared sandwiches, with chips and pickles. Cold drinks were in the refrigerator, and the bar was set up in the library if someone wished something stronger to drink. No one seemed to be hungry. The sandwiches remained under the plastic wrap, and the other items were left unopened. Coffee seemed to be the drink of choice. Lucy started a third pot.

Catherine had confided in Manny earlier in the day. She didn't mention that Hutch was alive, only that Pete had inadvertently stumbled into an identity theft ring on Amelia Island. He learned that the feds were monitoring the situation and SWAT teams were about to swarm the location. They also had a good idea where little Stephen was. Catherine asked Manny to give the officers forty-eight hours. She also told him that Pete thought the raid might be tonight and he was invited to join them as they waited for word that the operation netted the members of the ring.

Manny declined Catherine's invitation saying he thought he should stay at the department in case he was needed. Peaches was by his side. Fred and Brenda, and Pete and Tillie were maintaining the vigil by Catherine's side.

Catherine hadn't joined the group as yet, and Brenda was sure she knew where she could find her friend. She stepped up the winding staircase to the second floor and poked her head into the nursery. Catherine, sitting on the floor, leaning back against Stephen's crib holding a teddy bear, looked up and smiled at her dear friend.

"I thought I might find you here," Brenda said with a warm smile, as she sat on the floor next to Catherine.

"Brenda, I don't know which is harder, the day Stephen was abducted or today waiting to hear if he's safe and whether Hutch will be with me again."

"I don't know how you're holding it together, Catherine. I'd be a mess I'm sure."

Catherine looked at her watch. "Midnight. Let's go downstairs and join the others. I want to be near a phone."

—•••—

Catherine put out a puzzle in the dining room. She felt something mindless, something that did not require conversation, might be a good idea. She was right. Fred, Pete, and Tillie were at the table. Coffee cups contained varying levels of the stimulant—most near empty. Catherine and Brenda went to the kitchen to refill the carafe.

"Lucy, why don't you join us in the living room? I doubt anyone will be hungry until we hear something," Catherine said.

"Miss Catherine, I couldn't sit. But thank you anyway. I thought it would be a good time to clean out the pantry."

"Okay, but join us whenever you feel like it," Catherine said, giving her a hug. She understood how painful today was for Lucy who still blamed herself for allowing Stephen to be abducted in the first place.

Catherine and Brenda joined the others in the dining room, but Catherine couldn't sit down either. She walked over to the picture window, staring through the glass curtain. Turning to her friends at the table silently working on the puzzle, she asked, "Pete, did your friend JJ give you any idea as to when they would strike...early morning, late morning, or now, midnight?"

"No, he didn't, but my bet is it will be soon. They'll want the cover of darkness," Pete replied.

A shiver gripped Catherine as she turned and again stared out the window. "Please, dear God, let them both be safe," she whispered.

Chapter 48

—●●●—

AUGIE LAY IN BED, fully dressed. The house was quiet. Talib and Sayid had finally turned in a little after 11:30 p.m. He finished his text message to JJ, telling him exactly where everyone was bedded down. Talib and Sayid had private bedrooms on the first floor. Armed. Augie's bedroom was on the second floor and the three farmers were split in the two remaining bedrooms on the second floor in the back. One of the Tucson farmers was armed, the other two were not, and he was armed.

Watches were synchronized, checked, and double checked. SWAT teams assumed their positions. Each team's leader was equipped with a direct line to the commander. The only time they would hear from him was in the event they were to abort the operation. At 0215 EST they were to move in —Amelia Island, Detroit, and Montgomery. Tucson at 12:15 MST. Their rules of engagement—take everyone alive if possible. Fire only if necessary. However, it was believed that at least one person was armed at each location.

The SWAT team assigned to Tucson had a very tricky mission— extract Augie alive.

Chapter 49

—•••—

RETURNING TO HIS computer, Masud noticed a message on the center of his screen—"You have mail." Logging into his account he saw the new message was from his contact in Munich.

> "There was an Augustoff Weiss who lived out in the suburbs of Munich. He worked at a very sophisticated printing company but died two years ago in a plane crash. He was piloting the aircraft. There were no other passengers. Not much was written about the accident. His parents are deceased and there are no known relatives."

—•••—

It was now two o'clock in the morning. Masud's heart raced. Adrenalin poured through every fiber of his body. His brow wet with sweat. "Should I call Sayid," he asked himself, "or wait until morning? Don't be an idiot. It's just midnight in Tucson. I must call him now."

His hands shaking from the impact of what he had just learned—their whole network of farms was probably compromised—years of planning for nothing. "That stupid Layla," he ranted to himself, "she brought us bad luck. She was the one who suggested that Rafi should hire Augie...and then she grabbed that baby. Who knows, maybe she's in on it. She fled Amelia Island, leaving her brother, her teammates. She probably worked against them all along. Well her days are numbered. Rafi will have to kill her. Yes, he must kill Layla. That'll be a good lesson for the farmers. Traitors will not live to see another sunrise."

Masud, continuing to mutter to himself, kept punching the wrong numbers on his cell phone with his pudgy fingers. Finally, the call went through.

"Masud, why are you calling?" Sayid mumbled. "It is late. We all went to bed early because Talib is leaving in the morning."

"Sayid, he is a traitor," Masud yelled into the phone.

"Masud, calm down, I can hardly make out what you're saying. Say it again...slower. Don't yell."

"Augie, he's dead," he continued yelling. "There is no Augie. He—"

"Masud, what are you saying? Augie is a spy?" Sayid yelled back into the phone.

— •••—

Hutch's room was over Masud's. He heard the exchange. JJ heard the exchange through the bug.

Hutch sent a text to JJ:

> "I'M BURNED
> MOVE IN
> MOVE IN."

Chapter 50

—•••—

AT 2:12 AM EST, SWAT teams, dressed in black from head to toe, swarmed a house in Montgomery, Detroit and Fernandina Beach on Amelia Island. In each case, the farmers put up a fight. A farmer was killed on Amelia Island; a SWAT member was wounded in New York.

At the same time in Tucson, doors were kicked down, windows smashed, as the SWAT team swarmed the house. Sayid and Talib stumbled out of their bedrooms, guns blazing. They were taken out from behind by SWAT members entering through their bedroom windows. By the time they turned around to look backward, it was too late. Upstairs the three farmers bolted from their rooms. Caught by surprise by their friend Augie, the one armed farmer pulled his weapon but was stopped with a bullet through his wrist. Hutch held the three at bay as JJ bounded up the stairs followed by three more of his team.

They quickly cuffed the wrists of the two unarmed farmers as well as their feet. JJ yelled for a medic to treat the injured man.

Hutch ran downstairs and found Sayid and Talib in the hall. Sayid was dead. Talib was lying in a pool of blood, clutching his chest. His eyes full of hate focused on Hutch. Hutch knelt down to check his pulse. Talib gasping for breath said, "We will win. You cannot stop us."

"Talib, we just did stop you. Every farm has been seized," Hutch said—his lips close to Talib's ear.

Talib smiled. "New recruits will come...they will take their places...you will see...you will see," he whispered as life drained from his body.

Chapter 51

—•••—

THE PHONE RANG in Catherine's library. Startled, Catherine, lying on the couch trying to rest, sprang up. Pete laying back in the recliner pulled the lever returning him to an upright position. Catherine nodded to Pete to answer it. Reaching over to the lamp table beside him, he picked up the receiver.

"Hello."

"Is this Pete Peterson?"

"Yes, it is. JJ, is that you." Pete now sat on the edge of the recliner straining to be sure he heard every word.

"You got it, partner. Tell Catherine Hutch is safe."

"Here, I'm putting Catherine on the line. Please give her your message," Pete said, handing the phone to Catherine.

"Hello," Catherine said, her eyes closed, praying she would hear good news.

"We've never met, but I'm looking forward to changing that. You must be one helluva woman with what this guy's been through trying to get back to you."

"Is he...is Hutch okay?"

"Hang on. I'll let him tell you himself. Here he is."

"Hello, beautiful. Are you okay?"

"Oh, my sweetheart, yes...yes, I'm alright. What about Stephen?"

"Catherine...Stephen is missing but we believe he's in El Paso, at least that's where an agent picked up the woman who abducted him. JJ and I are on our way there now. I promise you I'll let you know as soon as we have some information."

"Be careful, my darling. God speed."

"Catherine, I love you...I won't stop until I find our son and bring him back to you safe and sound."

— •••—

"Well, Hutch, my friend, you don't look too much the worse for wear," JJ said turning the car into a private entrance at the Tucson airport.

"Just tell me where my son is. I have to believe he's okay. Layla came to look at him as her own, so I can't imagine she would let anyone hurt him," Hutch said straining to see the plane that would take them to El Paso.

"Baker tells me that Rafi hasn't said a word and Layla insists she doesn't know where he is," JJ replied.

"Well, they'd better start giving us some answers or I'll personally ensure they get a long stretch in prison."

"Now you're beginning to sound like my old partner in crime. See that sleek little jet over there?"

"I see it. I hope it's fast."

"The director himself ordered it up for us. Our first stop is El Paso and a heart-to-heart chat with Layla and Rafi. As you say, if they know what's good for them, they'll tell us where the little guy is." JJ led Hutch to the jet, its engine running. Seeing JJ and Hutch approach, the mechanic climbed down to the tarmac. "She's all yours, sir. Have a good flight."

The two men climbed aboard. "I'll fly the little bird to our first stop," JJ said. "So strap yourself in until after we take off. Then you'll find a change of clothes and a bag of toiletries in the back closet. I thought you'd like to cut that hair off and shave before you scare the love of your life to death. There's even a shower back there. I figure this baby will get us to El Paso in a little less than an hour."

At thirty-thousand feet, Augie shuffled to the rear of the plane. Taking a shower, the water beating down on him, he closed his eyes and once again said a prayer of thanks he was alive and another to please, dear God, let Catherine want him back in her life. After the shower, he fished out the hair clippers and gave himself a buzz cut and a clean shave. He put on the white golf shirt and black trousers JJ had purchased for him complete with black socks and loafers with tassels. Fishing around in the back pocket of the blood-spattered cargo pants he had worn, he pulled out the St. Christopher medal that Catherine had given him the night Stephen was conceived. Rubbing it softly between his fingers, he again prayed the medal would bring him good luck in finding the baby with the blonde hair and one little curl alive.

Slapping on the cologne he found in the bag, he took a look in the mirror. The transformation complete, he smiled at the man looking back at him. Putting his hands on the sink he bent his head down, overwhelmed at the thought of handing little Stephen to his mother, and then holding Catherine in his arms. Straightening up, he walked back to the front of the plane and took the co-pilot seat next to JJ.

"Wow, you clean up nice," JJ said.

"Thanks, JJ, for the clothes and other stuff."

"Now don't get all blubbery on me. We still have some serious work ahead of us. So, sit back and get some shut eye."

Chapter 52

—•••—

IT WAS ALMOST 9:30 in the morning. Manny sat at his desk, softly tapping a pencil on the calendar desk pad. Catherine had called to say the feds had moved successfully on the identity theft ring. She had then handed the phone to Pete who told him that the officers would be getting in touch with him. They wanted to see the evidence that Manny had gleaned about the various cars he'd tracked down. The agents were plugging the holes in their case.

Manny, inhaling slowly on the cigarette, continued to ponder over Catherine's actions the last few days. He was hurt she hadn't confided in him sooner. Peaches was lying on her pillow but she wasn't asleep. Her eyes were fixed on her master, sensing his malaise. The phone rang and Manny eased forward to answer it.

"Captain, the chief from Orlando PD is on line three. He asked for you specifically."

"Okay, Sergeant." Manny punched the button for line three. "Salinas."

"Hi, Captain. We met at the Orlando Airport that night when the Hainsworth child was kidnapped. Is the baby still missing? I haven't seen anything in the news for awhile."

"Yes, he's still missing. Why?"

"I just had a call from a convent in El Paso. A Sister Mary Margaret said a small child, a boy of about one, may be a few months older, was left at a nearby church with a note on him to call the Orlando Police Department."

"So, what makes you think there's a connection?" Manny leaned back in his chair.

"The note said the child had been taken at the Orlando Airport several weeks ago, and we have no other cases of this nature since the time when we met you with the mother at the airport."

Manny stood up, now gripping the phone. "Did you get the Sister's phone number? I don't know how he could have ended up in El Paso, but I'll certainly follow up. Thanks and I'll let you know what I find."

Manny immediately punched in the number the chief had given him.

"Hello, Benedictine Sisters. May I help you?"

"Yes, do you have a Sister Mary Margaret at your church?"

"I'm sorry, sir, you've reached the convent, but yes, Sister Mary Margaret does reside here."

"My name is Captain Salinas, from the Daytona Beach Police Department in Florida. The Sister placed a call to the Orlando Police Department a short while ago, regarding a young child, a boy, left at a church."

"Oh, my. Let me get Sister Mary Margaret."

"Hello, Captain Salinas?"

"I understand a little boy is in your custody."

"Oh, yes, Captain. An adorable little boy. His name is Stephen, if I'm not mistaken. At least that's what the note said. Do you know him? We're trying to find his family."

"Yes, yes, I know his mother and she's been frantic trying to find him. He was kidnapped at the Orlando Airport."

"Well, yes, sir, that is exactly what the note said."

"Sister Mary Margaret, I'm going to call his mother so she can speak to you directly. Is he all right?"

"He seems to be in wonderful condition. A hungry little guy, I will say that for him," she said with a light-hearted laugh.

— • • • —

"Hainsworth residence. Pete Peterson here."

"Well, Pete, have you taken up residency at Catherine's house?" Manny said with a touch of sarcasm. "Can I speak to Catherine?"

"Sure, Manny. Here she is."

"Manny, hello." Catherine heard the tension in her voice and perceived the same coming from the other end, although Manny hadn't said a word.

"Cat, I have what I think may be great news. I just talked with a nun, Sister Mary Margaret, in El Paso, Texas. A little boy was left at a church and given over to her at the convent. He had—"

"Manny, is it Stephen?" Catherine gasped into the receiver. Pete, standing in front of her, looked at her wide-eyed.

"I'm sure of it. I'll give you the number. I told the nun that you would call. Do you have a fax machine?"

"Yes, of course, in my studio."

"FAX Stephen's picture to her. She must have a fax, there, don't you think?"

"I would hope so. Oh, Manny, thank you, thank you, thank you." Catherine wrote the number on a pad, hung up the phone, and looked at Pete. Tears of joy trickled down her face melting into her smile. "Oh, Pete, a nun called from a convent in El Paso. She thinks she has Stephen."

—•••—

After talking with Sister Mary Margaret, and promising she was going to FAX some pictures right away, and thanking the nun again and again, Catherine removed the picture of Hutch and herself from the frame and dashed upstairs for the pictures of Stephen she had given to the press.

With Catherine again at his side, Pete punched in JJ's cell number. When JJ picked up, Pete asked him to hand the phone to Hutch.

"Pete, what's up? We are just about to land in El Paso."

"Hang on. Catherine has some news for you."

"Hutch, you aren't going to believe what just happened. Manny had a call that Stephen is at a convent in El Paso. Darling, he's okay. I talked with a Sister Mary Margaret and she went on and on at how cute he is, and that he's just fine. Pete's taking pictures I have of Stephen and one with you and me. He's sending them to JJ's cell. Hutch, I told Sister Mary Margaret that you're his father. You may need some identification...you'll have the pictures...I can't imagine she would just hand him—"

"My darling, I think I know someone who will make sure we don't have a problem. Give me the number of the convent and send the pictures. Catherine, I love you, I love you. Wait for my call that I have our son."

—•••—

Hutch punched in the private line to his boss. "Sir, I need your help. Please call the following number. It's a convent. Ask for Sister Mary Margaret, and let her know she can give the little boy in her custody to the man in the picture his mother just faxed to her. And tell her I'll be carrying a duplicate picture."

"My pleasure," the director replied. "And, Hutch, good job!"

Chapter 53

—•••—

TWO HOURS LATER Hutch and JJ entered the chapel of the Benedictine Sisters' convent. The soft glow emanating from the stained glass windows filled the quiet space with warmth.

Sister Mary Margaret stepped through the heavy oak door holding Stephen's chubby finger in an attempt to steady his little legs just getting the hang of walking. Stephen looked at Hutch for a second and then took several little running steps almost toppling over. "Daddy. Daddy."

"Oh, my God. Yes, Stephen, it's daddy," Hutch said sweeping the toddler up in his arms. He glanced over at JJ and then to Sister Mary Margaret with a quizzical look. "How did he know me? I don't look like his friend Augie with my hair cut and beard shaved."

"This picture I guess," the nun said. "His mother sent it to me and then a big man somewhere, I think he said he worked for the government, called to say it was all right to give the lad to you. He swore you were his father. Then he sent the same picture with a very pretty lady. Is she his mother?"

"Yes, she is," Hutch said swallowing hard several times, but a tear escaped his eye no matter how hard he tried to hold it back. JJ stepped forward holding his phone up so the nun could see the same picture on his cell.

"Well, it looks like you're going to be together again. I'd say this little one is a very lucky lad. God bless you, my son." Sister

Mary Margaret kissed the top of Stephen's wavy blonde head. "God speed."

Another sister stepped forward handing a small, dusty-blue duffel bag sporting a cartoon alligator to JJ. She kissed Stephen's rosy cheek, and stepped back, bowing her head as she did so.

"Sister, do you mind if I call his mother? I'm sure she would like to thank you personally for taking care of her son...our son," Hutch asked. Stephen now had his arms wrapped around Hutch's neck, his head nestled tight, sucking his thumb.

"Of course, I don't mind."

JJ had already punched in Catherine's number. This time she answered herself.

"Hi, Catherine. It's me, JJ, again. Here's Hutch."

"Hello, sweetheart. I'm holding our son...right now. Sister Mary Margaret is with us...yes, yes...here she is."

Hutch couldn't hear what Catherine said, but the sister smiled running her fingers over Stephen's blonde cap. "Bless you, my dear. I'm sure you're looking forward to their homecoming."

Chapter 54

— • • • —

THE JET, NOW over Florida, would soon begin its descent to land onto the Amelia Island airstrip. JJ called Pete to let him know they were approaching and would be on the ground in less than fifteen minutes, and, yes, the precious cargo was aboard—both of them.

Pete put his cell phone back in his pocket and turned to look into Catherine's questioning eyes.

"That was JJ. They'll be on the ground shortly. In less than fifteen minutes little Stephen will be in your arms, Catherine. Are you ready?"

"Oh, Pete, I am so ready. To think I will once again hold my little miracle in my arms... and Hutch coming back to me is...beyond wonderful. Let's go outside, I want him to see I'm welcoming him with open arms."

Brenda stepped forward, giving Catherine a hug. "Good luck, my friend."

"That goes for me too," Fred said, circling Brenda with his arm and planting a quick peck on Catherine's cheek.

"Hey, my darlin' Tillie and I will be waiting, giving you some time, not too long, to join you and my friend Hutch over drinks. He has some explaining I want to hear, and I do love to see him squirm," Pete laughed as he placed a kiss on Catherine's other cheek.

"That's a deal, my friends, after...what did you say, Pete, after we have some time?" Catherine gave a quick hug to each of her friends and then stepped out of the little building and onto the edge of the tarmac. Brenda and Fred, and Tillie and Pete followed but stayed in the background.

Looking to the west, Catherine shielded her eyes from the bright, late afternoon sun. "There. There. Is that their plane?" she asked, pointing up at the deep blue, cloudless sky.

A silver speck caught in the sun's rays, sparkled like a big star slowly descending over the trees. Setting the jet down softly on the runway, JJ brought the plane to a stop then turned and taxied within a few yards from where Catherine stood. Cutting the engines, he jumped out of the pilot's seat, opened the door, and flipped down the stairs.

Hutch picked up little Stephen and kissed him on the cheek. "Let's go see your mommy, little guy." Stephen wrapped his chubby arms around his daddy, gave him a kiss on the cheek and pulled back giggling.

Hutch wasn't sure his legs would hold him as he descended the stairs and saw Catherine, her white dress fluttering around her knees. She ran to him grasping little Stephen into her arms, but never taking her eyes, sparkling brightly with teardrops, away from Hutch. Hutch wrapped his arms around Catherine and their son in a tight embrace. "My darling, forgive me for doubting our love. Stephen is a wonderful little boy. Please let me raise my son with you."

"My handsome agent, that is exactly what I want you to do." With little Stephen clinging to Catherine, mother and father embraced...an embrace erasing the fears and tortured memories of the last year and a half.

Looking into Catherine's soft brown eyes filled with love, "There is one thing, Catherine."

"And what is that?" she asked, her face beaming.

"I don't want to be your agent. I want to be your husband...I want you to be my wife."

"I'm sure that can be arranged...and the sooner the better, my darling."

The End

REVIEW REQUEST

Dear reader, I hope you enjoyed meeting a new friend, Elizabeth Stitchway. If you have the time, it would mean a lot to me if you wrote a review, your honest appraisal. What did you like most? It's super easy. Go to Amazon. Log in. Search: <u>Mary Jane Forbes Choices</u>

Thank you!

Books by Mary Jane Forbes

FICTION

The Witness Series
The Fisherman, a love story
The Witness, living a lie

Murder by Design, Series:
Murder by Design
Labeled in Seattle
Choices, And the Courage to Risk

Novels
The Mailbox
Black Magic, An Arabian Stallion
The Painter
The Baby Quilt … a mystery!
The Message…Call Me!
Twister

House of Beads Mystery Series
Murder in the House of Beads
Intercept
Checkmate
Identity Theft

Short Stories
Once Upon a Christmas Eve, a Romantic Fairy Tale
The Christmas Angel and the Magic Holiday Tree

NONFICTION
Authors, Self Publish With Style

Visit: www.MaryJaneForbes.com